"I'm not sure one apology is going to be sufficient..."

"I make a mean chocolate-chip pancake," Mason offered, surprising her. "I could make you a replacement."

Somehow, Maddie didn't think his pancakes would be second best. Nope. Just like his smile, she had a feeling his pancakes would be addictive. He was a big, scary-looking guy offering homemade breakfast. Talk about checking all the right boxes.

"You cook," she blurted out. He was a chef at the resort, even if he wore camo pants, a black T-shirt and combat boots, and looked more like a badass than a cook.

"Yeah. I do. Really well. I take it that's a no on the pancake offer."

Actually, she wanted to scream yes, please, and not just for his pancakes.

"That's not what chefs wear." She flicked a finger up and down, indicating his clothes.

He grinned. "I'm not in the kitchen right now, sweetheart. I'm allowed to be out of uniform."

And now she was thinking about him naked...

Dear Reader,

The idea for *Pleasing Her SEAL* came to me when I was writing *Teasing Her SEAL*. I was in a panic, trying to come up with some kind of erotic, slightly-kinky-but-not-*too*-kinky fantasy that my heroine and her SEAL could bring to life. Apparently, my own life was rather boring and I was fresh out of fantasies that didn't involve tropical islands and certain notorious pirates. So I did what any self-respecting author does when she needs to fact-check something—I did a Google search. There are plenty of top-ten fantasy lists out there and more than one involved bringing food into the bedroom. Strawberries, champagne and body chocolate? Yes, please! Suddenly I had plenty of ideas for *Pleasing Her SEAL*.

We all want to be sexy and desirable—and we all have a few hidden fantasies. Wedding blogger Maddie Holmes is curvy and funny, with a mouth that won't stop and a definite sweet tooth. US Navy SEAL Mason Black is undercover as a resort chef on Fantasy Island. He's also on a mission to get close to Maddie—really, really close. Soon he's wooing her with whipped cream, frosting and a very naughty candy necklace.

I hope you enjoy Maddie and Mason's story! I'd love to hear from you—so stop by and visit me on Facebook and on Twitter, @anne_marsh.

Happy reading,

Anne Marsh

Anne Marsh

—

Pleasing Her SEAL

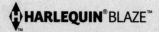

ISBN-13: 978-0-373-79879-7

Pleasing Her SEAL

Anne Marsh writes sexy contemporary and paranormal romances because the world can always enjoy one more alpha male. She started writing romance after getting laid off from her job as a technical writer—and quickly decided happily-ever-afters trumped software manuals. She lives in Northern California with her family and six cats.

Books by Anne Marsh

Harlequin Blaze

Uniformly Hot!

Wicked Sexy
Wicked Nights
Wicked Secrets
Teasing Her SEAL

To get the inside scoop on Harlequin Blaze and its talented writers, be sure to check out BlazeAuthors.com.

All backlist available in ebook format.

Visit the Author Profile page at Harlequin.com for more titles.

This one's for Gwen Hayes. Yes, again. Because no books get written without the awesomeness of Gwen and, when you read this, we'll be cruising the Caribbean and plotting literary world domination. We're going to be unstoppable.

1

Ladies, it's Saturday and I'm surrounded by honeymooners. This is one step up from my usual weekend wedding gig, where my people options are usually the geriatric crowd, the toddler dancing crowd (always good for a much-needed cardio burst and the cutest, stickiest kisses), or the drunken groomsman crowd (good for equally enthusiastic but much damper kisses—eww). I counted not one, not two, but *three* couples wrapped around each other by the pool. I have dubbed them the Octopi because they seem to have eight hands each and at least seven of them are engaged in activities best left to the bedroom or a soft porn channel. Go, Octopi! Speaking of that, watching the Octopi procreate underscores my own single state. You've found The One and you're hearing wedding bells, or you wouldn't be visiting this blog. Any tips for where to look for a good guy? Because this wedding blogger is feeling lonely in paradise.

—MADDIE, Kiss and Tulle

"Hooyah, hooyah, hooyah, hey." US Navy SEAL Mason Black fist-bumped his knuckles with Levi Brandon's. He didn't have far to reach since both men were currently sharing the same palm tree backrest and catching their breaths after completing their mission.

"Today's gonna be another easy day." Levi automatically finished the chant. The words took Mason back to BUD/S training when making the SEALs team had still been seven weeks of hell away. Operating on four hours of sleep or less a night, he'd worked with his teammates to carry their Zodiac over their heads through the pounding surf, crawled through mud flats and made best friends with a three-hundred-pound log that was their instructors' idea of exercise equipment. Good times.

Levi grinned as if he hadn't just been embroiled in a firefight. "I'm hoping there's a beer in my future."

The current op wasn't so bad and beat the hell out of completing the O course at BUD/S. Not only had the rain finally stopped, which went in the plus column, but one hell of a tropical sunrise lit up the horizon. Since he was waiting for the Zodiacs from the US Navy cruiser anchored just offshore, Mason had every reason to stare at the horizon. His team was minutes away from successfully finishing their undercover op on Fantasy Island.

One more checkmark in the "mission complete" column.

If he'd been a paperwork-and-spreadsheet kind of guy. Which he wasn't.

Nope, he mused to himself as he went to work with a SIG Sauer and a sniper rifle. Rather than riding the commuter train, he'd be extracted from the island by

Black Hawk and flown to the nearest US military base to debrief. And instead of writing quarterly reports or coding software, he'd helped lead the hostile extraction of a South American drug lord who'd made the mistake of booking a luxury vacation for himself and his new girlfriend on Fantasy Island.

Mason's SEAL team had moved in early, posing as resort staff, and intercepted the guy as soon as he'd stepped foot on the island. Pretending to be a gourmet chef had actually been fun. Poolside ceviche lessons were a nice change of pace from dodging bullets, and he genuinely liked cooking. The female students weren't bad looking, either.

SEAL Team Sigma had established an undercover camp on Fantasy Island's undeveloped side. Unlike the resort digs, their camp was basic. A few hammocks, a couple of tents and enough hardware and weaponry to take over a small country. They could be packed and wheels up in two hours, and that portability alone made the place more perfect than a country club. Better yet, the rugged terrain all but guaranteed that no resort guest would stumble across the SEALs.

The faint sound of Zodiacs cutting across the lagoon announced that it was showtime. Diego Marcos, the captured drug lord, started cursing up a storm behind his duct-tape gag and pulling at his zip-tied wrists. The scumbag wasn't going to quit until he was in US custody aboard the Navy vessel cruising offshore, and maybe not even then. Not Mason's problem. The girlfriend, however, looked peaked and more than a little teary, so Mason helped her to a seat on the sand with a hand under her elbow.

She might or might not know squat about her beau's

drug-running activities, but she'd come here with him and now she was tarred with the same brush. Marcos shot her a look, not quite managing to mask his concern. Mason got that. Separating your personal life from your professional life was hard.

Mason didn't like the worry in her eyes, either, so when she stared up at him, he broke out his Spanish for Dummies. *"No te preocupes que vas a estar bien."*

The way her eyes welled up at his words wasn't a good sign. Or maybe she'd just had enough. Someone, somewhere was going to miss her. That unknown someone would want to yell at her for her bad choice in men and then maybe add an "I told you so." He could imagine all too easily how he'd feel if she was one of his sisters or his cousins, seven females he loved more than life itself and who'd managed, collectively, to date every badass bad guy out there. Some of them more than once.

He tucked a loose strand of hair behind her ear and fell back. He couldn't let her go, and he couldn't give her a do-over. So the best thing was to get out of her personal space.

"Softie," Levi mouthed.

Yeah, but he was also the softie in charge at the moment. Their team leader, Gray Jackson, was supervising the medevac of an injured team member, so Mason had command.

Something flashed at his nine o'clock. Light on glass, like a camera lens. Typical. Right when the mission wrapped and they were all free to ride off into the sunset, everything went FUBAR. Lifting his binoculars, he zoomed in and, damn, it was the hot chick who'd attended the cooking lessons. She'd liked his ceviche. He'd liked…her.

She was gorgeous, with a smile that lit her up from the inside out, radiant red hair bouncing around her shoulders. During the class, she'd worn a polka-dot sundress with tiny straps crisscrossing her shoulders, and his new mission had become finding a way to nudge those thin ribbons down her shoulders and get to know her. Biblically.

He nudged Levi with the toe of his boot. "We've got company."

"Tell me it's the Budweiser truck."

"We're on an island, dumbass."

"Don't be so literal." Levi saluted him with his middle finger. "And let a man dream. Where's our hot spot?"

"Up on the hill. Nine o'clock. We've got a resort guest out and about."

Levi snatched the glasses away from him and examined the hillside. "You're not wrong," he said. "Jogger?"

"No such luck. That's Madeline Holmes. She's a wedding blogger and right now she's snapping pictures of the lagoon."

She was also his personal eye candy, her happy-go-lucky smile drawing his attention every time he was near her. And if he'd taken advantage of this island op to put himself in her vicinity as often as possible, that was need-to-know information.

"And in another ten, our pickup crew." Levi cursed. "Options?"

Their mission was already FUBAR in some respects: Remy taking a bullet to the abdomen and being

airlifted to a hospital, Gray bleeding emotionally because he'd taken a header for the visiting doctor who'd
flown out with the injured SEAL. Pick one. Hell, pick
both. This was why an insertion into civilian space
spelled danger. Everything was easier in the jungle.
Something moved, you shot it. Not, of course, that he
wanted to shoot the woman.

"What are the odds she's taking selfies?" Levi asked.

Zero to none. A familiar calm descended. His pretty
redhead was a threat to his team, so he'd neutralize her.
No matter how alive she made him feel, the mission
and the team came first. "I'll take care of it. You hand
off our guests here to the Navy boys."

"Got it." Levi turned toward the approaching Zodiac. "Try to remember that we're on a no-kill mission,
okay? Plus, she's friends with Ashley, and you don't
want to piss off Ashley."

Jesus. Did he look that cranky? Or like the kind
of guy who would take out an innocent civilian? He
agreed with the warning on Ashley Dixon, though.
She was a DEA loaner and honorary member of the
SEAL team—and she could be mean as hell if you riled
her up. Moving rapidly, he stripped off his more obvi-
ous weapons and dropped them on the sand. Since he
was supposed to be undercover, working on the down
low, he couldn't show up toting forty pounds of lethal
hardware.

MORNINGS SUCKED. PREDAWN ALARMS sucked even more
because no one, ever, had accused Madeline Holmes
of being a morning person. Still, she'd given it a shot,
scrambling up the hill even as she willed the sunrise

to hold off. Hitting the snooze button the third time had been a mistake.

In order to make the sunrise, she'd rolled out of bed and settled for a tank top, shorts and sneakers. Usually, she put some thought into her clothes. Okay. Lots of thought. Clothing was like armor. *Pretty* armor. Instead of rocking her suitcase full of brand-new vacation wear, however, she was climbing Mount Everest. She hadn't shaved her legs or brushed her hair and she stank of eau de bug spray.

Go, her.

As the air lightened around her, she pushed harder because the sun was coming up fast and, color her romantic, but she wanted to catch the first rays of dawn, the colors exploding over the edge of the horizon. This was probably her one and only chance to visit a place like Fantasy Island, so every moment needed to count—and the pictures would be awesome blog material. And the more footage she got, the better. Everything rode on this trip.

She was lucky to be here, even if she'd come alone. The Fantasy Island marketing team had reached out to her about advertising on her blog and, ka-ching, she'd found herself here on an all-expenses-paid vacation. Now she had to earn her keep or her chance at big-time success would go poof.

The place was paradise, so how hard could it be to talk the island up on her blog? The only thing missing was the naked hot guy. Or loincloth-wearing hot guy. She preferred a man of mystery to a letting-it-all-hang-out-in-the-breeze guy. If she'd understood the island's advertising correctly, she might be able to have her choice of either. Or both.

Whatever she wanted.

Fantasy Island advertised itself as an idyllic slice of paradise located on the Caribbean Sea—the perfect place for a destination wedding or honeymoon. The elegant type on the resort brochure promised barefoot luxury, discreet hedonism and complete wish fulfillment. Maddie's job was to translate those naughty promises into sexy web copy that would drive traffic to her blog and fill her bank account with much-needed advertising dollars.

The summit beckoned and she stepped out into a small clearing overlooking the ocean.

"I need to work out more." At least her asthma hadn't kicked in. After a quick check of the camera that she'd set up yesterday to do time-lapse photography, she unwrapped her breakfast. She had a purloined croissant and a mocha, which was the perfect sunrise-watching food. While she munched and she shot, the air lightened around her, the birds and the howler monkeys competing to see who could make the most raucous noise. Being awake this early was…almost okay.

The noise of a boat coming in hard and fast on the quiet side of the island was a surprise. With her camera lens, she zoomed in on a pair of black rubber dinghies bouncing over the lagoon's calm surface. *Huh.* She squinted, trying to make out the details. Not only did the guys riding the Zodiac look mean, but they were toting a small arsenal, too.

"Good view?" At the sound of the deep male voice behind her, Maddie flinched, arms and legs jerking in shock. Her camera flew forward as she scrambled backward. As adrenaline surged through her, she sucked in air—*happy place, happy place*—but her lungs betrayed her anyhow, her airway closing up tight. It felt like an elephant had parked its ass on her chest.

Strong male fingers fastened around her wrist. Panicked, she grabbed her croissant and lobbed it at the guy, followed by her coffee. He cursed and dodged.

"It's not a good day to jump without a chute." He tugged her away from the edge of the lookout, and she got her first good look at him. Not a stranger. *Okay, then*. Her heart banged hard against her rib cage, pummeling her out-of-air lungs, before settling back into a more normal rhythm. *Mason*. Mason I-Can't-Be-Bothered-To-Tell-You-My-Last-Name-But-I'm-A-Stud. He led the cooking classes by the pool. She'd written him off as good-looking but aloof, not certain if she'd spotted a spark of potential interest in his dark eyes. Wishful thinking or dating potential—it was probably a moot point now, since she'd just pegged him with her croissant, followed by her mocha. Usually she couldn't hit the broad side of a barn, but she'd scored a bull's-eye on the front of his T-shirt.

She sneaked a peek at him. He didn't seem pissed off. On the contrary, he simply rocked back on his haunches, hands held out in front of him. *I come in peace*, she thought, fortunately too out of breath to giggle. The side of his shirt sported a dark stain from her coffee. Oh, goody. She'd actually scalded him. Way to make an impression on a poor, innocent guy. This was why her dating life sucked.

She tried to wheeze out an apology, but he shook his head.

"Let's get you breathing."

She had to agree with his priorities. Plus, if he wanted her breathing, he clearly hadn't morphed from resort chef to serial killer, so he had some other reason for being up here. Who knew? Maybe he was a secret sunrise aficionado. With a grimace, she dumped her bag upside down on the ground, looking for the inhaler hiding somewhere in the mountain of stuff she carted around. Mason made a choked sound, but she ignored him. So she had a *lot* of stuff. Preparation was the key to surviving, right? Plus, she really, really hated cleaning out her bag. Mason rifled through the contents, his fingers skimming over her secret chocolate stash, mini samples from her Birchbox subscription, three pairs of sunglasses, a paperback and a clear plastic pouch of emergency tampons. Since he didn't look as if he wanted to run back down the hill screaming, she concentrated on breathing.

"Got it." Uncapping her inhaler, he handed it to her. Dark brown eyes watched her as she primed the device and shoved it into her mouth. "I scared you."

"You think?" The albuterol went to work, her lungs opening up like her puffer was a magic wand and she'd just chanted *open sesame*. She hated having to rely on the device, but sometimes she couldn't talk herself out of panicking.

"That wasn't my intention." The look on his face was part chagrin, part repentance. Worked for her.

"I'll put a bell around your neck." Where had he learned to move so quietly?

"Why don't we start over?" He stuck out a hand. A big, masculine, slightly muddy hand. She probably shouldn't want to seize his fingers like a lifeline. "I'm Mason Black."

"I know who you are." Or mostly. The last name was new information.

Belatedly, she shoved her hand into his. Good Lord, the man had her acting as though she was fifteen. Not that she'd mind having her fifteen-year-old body back, but that year in high school had been the Year of Brody. Brody had sat next to her in her chemistry class, his mere presence driving textbooks straight out of her mind and reducing her to a stammering, drooling idiot. He'd made her tingle and flush, transforming chemistry class into both her favorite and her worst period of the day.

Mason Black was even more devastating. And, like her chemistry crush, she wasn't entirely positive he knew her name. After all, he'd just introduced himself to her as if they were total strangers and she hadn't ogled his body while he taught Fantasy Island's guests to make ceviche. Which she totally had.

She was also still holding his hand.

Oops. Letting go, she took a step back.

"I'm Maddie Holmes."

"Uh-huh." He cleared his throat. "I owe you an apology."

She leaned toward him before she could stop herself. "Okay."

Did she still sound breathless? Maybe she could blame her asthma. He examined the ground and her gaze followed his. Right. Her camera…and her breakfast. Her breakfast was beyond repair—even she wasn't going to eat a chocolate croissant that had bounced off Hot Chef's chest and hit the jungle floor—but her camera was a different story. He picked it up, turned it over in his hands and then handed it to her.

"The first apology is for scaring you. It wasn't intentional." His lips curved up in a grin. "And the second apology is for your camera. And your croissant." She liked the slow way he smiled at her. It made her feel all melty, like the insides of her croissant.

"It was chocolate," she pointed out. "One apology may not be sufficient."

"Call me crazy, but aren't cameras a bit more expensive than breakfast pastries?"

"I have more than one camera," she explained. "But at the moment, I'm completely croissant-less."

"I make a mean chocolate-chip pancake," he offered, surprising her. With that brawny body, she'd assumed he was an oat bran and protein powder kind of guy. "I could make you a replacement."

Somehow, she didn't think his pancakes would take second place. Nope. Just like his smile, she had a bad feeling his pancakes would be addictive. He was a big, scary-looking guy offering homemade breakfast. Talk about checking all the right boxes.

"You cook," she blurted out when the silence stretched on too long, and then wanted to smack herself. *Duh*. Obviously, he cooked. He was a chef at the resort, even if he wore camo pants, a black T-shirt and combat boots, and looked more like a badass than a chef.

"Yeah," he agreed, rocking back on his heels to survey her, presumably for further damage. "I do. Really well, although I'm hearing a *no* on my offer."

Only because she was biting her lip. She wanted to scream "yes, please" and not just for his pancakes.

"That's not what chefs wear." She flicked a finger up and down, indicating his clothes.

He grinned. "I'm not in the kitchen right now, sweetheart. I'm allowed to be out of uniform."

And now she was thinking about him naked.

"I'm playing paintball with some of the guys," he continued.

"At dawn?"

He shrugged. "You all like to eat. I have a job to do most of the time."

"You don't have any paint on your shirt." Although if his alleged teammates had hit him on the butt, she'd be happy to check out that portion of his anatomy, too.

He sighed. "That's because I'm good."

Again...maybe. Not that he had any reason to lie to her about paintball, but she had a suspicious nature. She tried to peer over his shoulder, but it was roughly the size of a small tree and offered plenty of places for a gal to dig in. His black T-shirt clung to him in all the right places, and black and green paint streaked his face. The colors drew attention to the strong line of his jaw and a really great pair of brown eyes.

She was staring.

Shoot.

"I saw boats." She pointed to the lagoon over his shoulder. "Two of those black inflatable dinghy things."

He turned around, crossing his arms over his broad chest. That move pulled the shirt tight. Since she was an equal-opportunity kind of gal, she checked out his ass, too. Which was tight and firm, unlike hers. She definitely needed to take up paintball.

He shrugged and pointed to the dinghy-less, bad-guy-less lagoon. "There's no one there now."

"But there was." She hated mysteries.

"It could be the Belizean police doing a routine drug check. They patrol up and down the coastline, and we're only a few miles offshore."

That sounded feasible. On her last visit to Cancun,

back when she'd had vacation time, benefits and a nine-to-five job, she'd spotted AK-47–toting Mexican police patrolling the beaches. The hotel had assured her that was standard operating procedure, although she'd almost choked on her margarita the first time she'd spotted the patrols. She stared at the camera in her hands.

"I have photos," she said.

"I didn't say I didn't believe you," he pointed out. "But I'm happy to look at anything you want to show me."

That almost sounded like a double entendre, but he said the words with a straight face, making it impossible to be sure. Instead, she focused on her camera and— damn it—its trip to the ground hadn't done it any favors.

"The memory card's gone. It must have popped out when I dropped the camera."

And flown over the edge, she decided a few minutes later, on its way down, down, down for a tropical swim. Mason helped her look, but the card was nowhere to be found. Of course, since she was searching for a teeny piece of plastic in the great outdoors, her odds hadn't been high to start with.

"I'm thinking I owe you more than a short stack," he said with a grimace. "Now you've lost your pictures, too."

This was where being prepared came in handy. "Not really. I had the camera set up to do time-lapse, and all the shots should have been transferred to my laptop if the Wi-Fi isn't moving on island time."

"Good to know," he muttered, his eyes on the camera in her hands. "What were you shooting?"

"Not what you were shooting." When he gave her a lopsided grin, she told him the truth. "Sunrise pictures.

Romantic stuff for my wedding blog. Brides will love having their pictures taken up here. I'm shadowing a wedding later this week, and the bride already picked out this spot for her photos. They're a gorgeous couple."

She whipped open her planner and flipped to the section where she'd jotted down her notes for the beach wedding. There were certain shots she definitely wanted to make sure she captured, and she did better with a list.

"This is my bride and groom. He's a hottie. My blog readers will love him."

Mason took the groom's picture from her. "This is your guy?"

"Uh-huh." She'd been in correspondence with Julieta, the bride, more than once before she'd arrived. The Mrs. Guzman-to-be was a pretty blonde, while her groom had the Mr. Tall, Dark and Handsome part down. He rocked a white linen suit in the photo Julieta had sent to give Maddie an idea of what they'd be wearing and, if he showed up looking like that, her photos would be outstanding. "What do you think?"

Mason snorted. "Not my type, sweetheart."

She stuck her tongue out at him. "Well, Mr. Guzman clearly appeals to the future Mrs. Guzman, and that's all that counts."

"They here on the island already?" He returned the photo and she stuck it back in her planner.

"Not yet." Which was both surprising and not. "Julieta's dress is here—that's the bride-to-be—but I haven't actually seen them check in yet. Mr. Guzman runs some kind of import-export business and has stuff come up at the last minute all the time. Maybe he had a business thing. It must be nice to have a private plane and go where you want, when you want."

"Maybe." Mason gestured at her tripod. "You done here? Want a hand bringing this back to your villa?"

"A hand down the hill would be great," she said, still thinking about her missing bride and groom. She'd been counting on shooting their wedding for her blog; if they were no-shows, she'd need to make alternative arrangements. "Maybe I'll see if his brother has arrived yet. Ask him if Mr. Guzman's plans have changed."

Mason started breaking down her tripod. "He's bringing family to his wedding?"

She shrugged. "Just his brother, Santiago, according to Julieta. He was planning to get to the island a few days before her, so she was hoping to pawn some of the prewedding tasks off on him. He should have arrived yesterday or today."

She let him help her fold up the tripod, and then they headed toward the path that led back to the resort. Since the sun had risen, the lighting was no longer ideal, and she now had a date with her bed. A date that would be even better if Mason followed her home. *No.* He wasn't a stray puppy. She didn't get to bring him home.

He strode ahead of her, so she followed along, admiring the way his cargo pants bunched over his butt as he walked. What he didn't know wouldn't hurt him—and she'd definitely take a rain check on those pancakes.

2

WHEN THEY REACHED the base of the hill, Mason called squad halt on the operation. Maddie had given him permission to lead her down the hill, and down the hill only, so he handed over the tripod and flashed her a quick salute.

She blinked at him, taking the tripod automatically. "Uh. Thanks." Her gaze dipped to the coffee stain on his shirt, her face radiating embarrassment. "Sorry about that. And about scalding you."

She turned pink as if he were actually bothered by a few ounces of hot coffee. He'd been shot at, pinned down and ambushed more times than he could count. Coffee was the least of his worries, although her blush was cute.

"No worries, sweetheart. See you around?"

"Pancakes," she answered, sounding slightly breathless, and he couldn't hold back his grin. God, she was fun. When she went left, he hung back. Partly just to watch her go because, hell yeah, he enjoyed the sassy swing of her hips. Maybe she was trying to drive him crazy. It was a possibility.

Mr. Guzman, his ass.

The groom-to-be in Maddie's photo was Diego Marcos and he would be arriving precisely never. His reservation had been canceled, courtesy of SEAL Team Sigma. The possibility of Marcos's brother showing up on Fantasy Island, however, was an unpleasant wrinkle that he'd need to alert the rest of the SEAL team to. If they didn't have intel on where the brother was, they needed to get it stat.

And added bonus… If Maddie ever found out what Mason had done, he'd be on her shit list for more reasons than scaring the bejesus out of her.

He opened his hand and looked down. He'd taken advantage of her panic to pop the memory card out of her very expensive camera. He'd always used an inexpensive point-and-shoot himself, but then his usual model was a dead enemy target that needed documenting. Sunrises clearly required better technology.

Unfortunately, boosting her memory card might not have been enough. If she'd transferred pictures via the resort's Wi-Fi, he had a bigger problem than the square of plastic in his hand.

By the time he'd made it back to their base camp, the prisoners were long gone on the Zodiacs, and the rest of the SEAL team was waiting for him. He'd take camping over five-star luxury resorts any day. The entire team, minus Remy, who was now somewhere between here and Belize, was present.

Gray nodded acknowledgment when Mason stepped into the campsite. Gray was one of the biggest SEALs Mason had ever met. The team's standing joke was that Gray didn't parachute out of the plane so much as he plummeted. Like a rock. Although he sprawled at ease on a pile of backpacks, there was nothing casual about the glance he raked over Mason. Blood stained his camo. He'd stayed with the injured Remy until the medevac lifted off.

Mason was last to arrive at the debriefing about to start. It was standard operating protocol to review every mission, identifying areas of concern where they could improve next time. The team sat in a semicircle, their attention focused on Gray. As soon as Mason dropped to the ground next to Levi, Gray reviewed the mission that they had just completed, beginning with their target's arrival on Fantasy Island and ending with Remy's medevac to Belize for emergency surgery. Since Gray's maybe-girlfriend Laney Parker was a surgeon and she'd accompanied Remy on the flight, Mason figured his teammate had a fighting chance.

When Gray finished the medical update and Levi had confirmed Marcos's handoff to the US Navy, Gray dropped a new bombshell. "We're not done here," he said.

"We get to vacation for real? Hooyah." Levi leaned forward. "I'm borrowing your black AmEx, Mason."

"Dumbass," Sam said. Their field medic was a laid-back Alabama boy, but his lean build and easy smile were deceptively mellow. He could kick butt with the best of them, and no one on the team swam faster or blew more stuff up. "He means you get to work overtime."

Gray shook his head. "Real mature, Sam. And accurate. Our mission parameters have changed. We were charged with bringing in Diego Marcos, but now we've got a second target. Marcos has a brother, who operates as his right-hand man."

"Would that be Santiago Marcos?" Maybe Maddie had it wrong. Maybe she *wasn't* planning to shoot the wedding of a notorious drug dealer who, according to her, had invited his equally notorious younger brother to the celebration.

Gray eyed him. "Are you psychic? Or is there something else we need to know about? Levi already mentioned that you hit a snag earlier today."

Maddie was definitely a complication. A beautiful, very alluring complication.

"We had a resort guest up on the hillside lookout spot." The place had some froufrou name like Lovers Lookout. He didn't think Gray needed to know that, or that the spot apparently starred front and center in Maddie's bridal portfolio. "She had a camera."

Gray scrubbed a hand over his head. "How long was she up there? Did she shoot the Zodiacs coming in?"

Yeah, but that was only the first problem in a long list. "The guest is Madeline Holmes. She's a blogger, one of those girls who hangs with Ashley."

Ashley waved a hand. "Maddie runs Kiss and Tulle. She covers destination weddings, wedding favors, wedding cakes, wedding dresses. Last month her blog had over two hundred thousand unique visitors."

"In other words, any noun that can be modified by the adjective *wedding*," Levi interrupted. Mason was willing to bet that Levi wouldn't recognize a wedding blog—or a wedding anything—if it bit him on the ass.

Ashley made a face. "Pretty much."

"Well, today she was covering sunrises." He had no idea why a bride would want to hike up a hill at dawn in her dress for a few photos, but far be it from him to judge. "And she set up her camera yesterday to do time-lapse photography."

"She likes to vlog," Ashley said with a sigh. "And live post."

Whatever *vlogging* was, he'd bet it was a security risk because Ashley made another face.

Gray cursed. "Give me options."

"I snagged her media card, but she claimed she'd already transferred her pictures over the resort's Wi-Fi."

Ashley leaned forward. "I've been monitoring traffic in and out, but she'll likely keep copies on her laptop. Unfortunately, our resident wedding blogger has been experimenting with time-lapse photography. Even more unfortunately for us, her photos got picked up by a national travel site."

Ashley flipped her tablet around, exhibiting a series of sunrise photographs shot over the pier. The first half dozen shots were harmless unless you had a thing against waves and pretty colors. The next-to-last picture, however, was a problem. It showed a Zodiac shooting through the opening in the reef and heading toward the dock. Mason had a bad feeling that if he zoomed in, he'd see Marcos's bodyguards bouncing over the water in that Zodiac. Worse, there was no sign of the Zodiac tied up to the dock in the next and final frame. The boat had disappeared in the thirty minutes between shots.

Gray nodded slowly. "We need to see what else she got."

"There's more," Mason said. "Maddie mentioned she was planning on shooting a wedding later this week and the bride's and groom's pictures are a match for Diego Marcos and Julieta Ortiz. She's been emailing

Julieta and she expected them to show up yesterday. She doesn't know their real names, but she knows their faces."

Gray pointed to Ashley. "Have the resort notify Maddie that the wedding has been canceled."

Ashley nodded. "Got it."

"She also mentioned Santiago," Mason divulged. He relayed what she'd told him about Santiago coming to the island to attend his brother's wedding. "What do we know about him, and do we have confirmation on his current whereabouts?"

"He could have been part of the advance team we took out. I'll reach out to command and see what they've got for us. In the meantime, no one breaks cover until we've got a bead on where Santiago is currently. Mason, you stick by Maddie's side. Use the time to find out exactly what she has—or doesn't have—on her laptop and to re-verify the identities of the other guests on the island. Make sure no one slipped past us, because if Santiago *is* here, he knows that Diego isn't and that's a problem."

"Smash and grab on the laptop?" Levi stepped up like he was ready to volunteer.

"Do I need to define *undercover* for you?" Gray crossed his arms over his chest. "You steal or break her laptop, and she's got a problem that becomes our problem. How much crime do you think there is on a luxury private island? The first people she's going to point a finger at will be staff."

"We could bring her in," Mason suggested reluctantly. "Interview her. Or ask US Customs to intercept her on her return trip."

If Maddie had had her camera trained on the lagoon

overnight, there was a very good chance she'd captured faces. Given what even amateur photo-editing software could do these days, leaving any images in Maddie's hands was a security risk. Put it together with the rest of her vlogging and… Diego's brother could connect the dots. Plus, if Santiago was here, Maddie could ID him, and he'd bet Santiago had come undercover if he'd come at all.

Gray nodded, apparently coming to the same conclusion. "Worst-case scenario, that works. The customs boys can seize her laptop and go over it, although she'll be asking questions."

"Okay, then, let's go with plan A. I'll find out what she's got. *If* she's got anything." For some reason, he wanted to play nice. After all, he'd already scared her once, and she'd almost hyperventilated on the spot. She was a civilian, not collateral damage.

Ashley examined her fingernails. "She's here for another week."

Good to know the timeline.

"I'll make sure she didn't record anything." If she had, Mason would wipe whatever device it was.

Gray frowned. "Be discreet, okay? Scrub her media and shadow her in case there's any blowback from Diego's people or Santiago."

Levi whistled as the meeting broke up. "You just scored bodyguard duty. Enjoy."

Playing bodyguard wasn't exactly the worst job in the world. He was all for sticking as close as possible to Maddie—up to and including getting naked. *No. Wait. Resist that thought, sailor.*

Ashley rummaged in her bag. "I'm helping, too."

"Really?" Levi smirked, and even Mason recognized condescension when it stared at him. "How are you going to do that?"

Ashley pointed to Mason. "Penis angle." And then she pointed to herself. "Girlfriend angle."

"You think Maddie's going to make *Mason* her new boy toy?"

Mason punched Levi in the shoulder when his teammate snorted. Sure, he was an introvert and no flirt, but he'd dated as recently as this year. He didn't need Levi's lousy dating advice. The guy had a different woman for each day of the week, and he seemed perfectly happy that way. But that wasn't the way Mason planned on living his life.

"Read this." Ashley shoved a magazine into his hands. The cover was one of those bright pink numbers with a too-perfect model. A brunette with spectacular boobs, her hair flying in an artificial breeze while she gave the camera a come-hither face.

No, thank you. "This is waiting room material."

Ashley grinned at him. "Maddie has a serious magazine addiction. She loves the quizzes, so think of this as enemy intel. X marks the spot, big guy."

He paged through the magazine. He'd been on the receiving end of intel more than once and it had never smelled like perfume before, or—he paused—scratch-and-sniff ads for tropical air fresheners. When he hit Ashley's Post-it note, he stopped reading.

"You think I should take a quiz on how to be the perfect guy?"

Mason had four sisters. Surely that ought to qualify him as something of a girl expert? His jaw tightened. On the other hand, he'd also been married and divorced, so his credentials were rocky.

Ashley slapped his shoulder. "Read it. Then ask questions."

Since Ashley had to be one of the most tenacious people Mason knew, he read. It was quicker that way. And she was right—it wouldn't hurt to find out what it took to be a keeper guy. Mason's sisters loved that crap. So did his cousins. A road map couldn't hurt. He read the first quiz question.

You kiss her for the first time. After you break your lip-lock, you:

A) Tell her you've been fantasizing about kissing her for days—and that the reality is even better than the fantasy.

B) Whisper that she's the hottest kisser ever— and you've got a list of other places you'd like to kiss her.

C) Praise her kissing skills and beg her to do it again just so you can be sure.

Jesus. What had happened to just kissing? "This stuff works?"

Levi ripped the quiz out and tucked it into the pocket of Mason's pants. "Take notes and have fun, sailor."

3

This girl might just have the best job in the world! I'm hanging out on a tropical island, the cocktails are free and hotness is a basic job requisite. Because did I mention the good-looking guys are everywhere? Yum. I even ran into a bona fide single guy yesterday and he's got yours truly thinking that a vacation fling should be part of my plans. Fantasy Fodder— let's call him FF for short—accidentally bumped into me when I was snapping you some gorgeous photos of the lagoon at sunrise (ladies, you're *totally* going to want to do your wedding photos here, although I recommend a less obscene hour than the ass crack of dawn). Then he jumped right into rescue mode and kept yours truly from going over the edge of the cliff. So there I am with my very own white knight and rescue hottie, and he's not even mad that I may have christened him with a venti white mocha. A guy with a sense of humor and strong, manly hands? Sign me up, ladies!

—MADDIE, Kiss and Tulle

THERE NEEDED TO be a fourth, hidden option for people who wanted to increase their odds of hooking up because Maddie wasn't an A, B or C girl. Her generous coating of SPF-100 sunscreen—*thanks, Mom, for the redheaded gene*—and a blue-and-white-checked retro two-piece definitely didn't fall into the string-bikini category, although the buttons marching down her hips were a sassy touch she loved. She also appreciated her curves, even if they didn't always fit into a standard-issue bikini. There was a whole lot of her recently thanks to a post-layoff diet of wedding cake and favors. She needed to plan on buying new clothes or minimizing the sweets.

A mental image of Mason popped into her head. He'd be anything *but* sweet. *Bad girl.* Maybe she'd been single long enough to recover from her last disastrous relationship or maybe it was something about Fantasy Island itself, because the resort certainly encouraged her erotic daydreams with their hunky help. She'd posted about her hot man on a hillside early this morning. If she couldn't get an orgasm from him, she'd at least get a blog post. So far, the yeas outnumbered the nays two to one in her "Would you have hot vacation sex?" poll.

Since it was the low season, Fantasy Island didn't have many guests at the moment. There had only been two other women on the seaplane that had brought her here. Laney Parker had been using up her honeymoon reservation after her fiancé had ditched her, and Ashley Dixon had won a free getaway in some sort of Facebook contest. The low occupancy was undoubtedly the reason why Fantasy Island's owners had been willing to fly her here free so she could blog about their awe-some resort offerings.

This was her big break. If Fantasy Island bought banner advertising on her blog, she'd be able to keep the lights on in her condo for at least six more months… and having one high-profile client would attract others. Business was like dating. The more popular a girl was, the more guys lined up to buy her drinks and share their contact info. So far, her blog had been a wallflower, but she was determined that those lonely days were over.

And writing about the pool scene was certainly no hardship. The pool itself was all sleek curves. Private cabanas offered guests superb views of the sea, and staff moved discreetly among the loungers, offering fruit kebobs and Evian water spritzes. Ashley waved from a cabana. She wore an electric-pink string bi-kini and held a paperback that almost outweighed her.

Ashley shoved her sunglasses up on top of her head. "Are you here for the cooking lesson?"

Not intentionally, but it sounded like fun, particu-larly if it came with a side of Mason. She dropped onto the cushion beside Ashley, taking care not to slosh the mango margarita she'd acquired at the bar.

"I could be," she agreed. "I like free food."

Ashley nodded. "We're making mango-raspberry crepes with honeyed goat cheese."

Yeah, that sounded pretty good. "I'm in," she de-cided.

And then, wouldn't you know it, Mason strode to-ward the pool, and he was the cherry on the sundae. He wore black linen plants that clung to his muscular thighs as he moved. Instead of looking silly in the white chef's jacket and hat, he looked in control. Confident.

He'd rolled his sleeves up, revealing powerful forearms. She was almost certain she was holding her breath, damn it. He was just one guy. One really hot, supersexy guy. His dark gaze slid over her, stopped, and he nodded. She had no idea what that meant. *Hi? Glad to see you? Wait, there's the woman I almost knocked over a cliff?* The man should come with a secret decoder ring.

Ashley sat up cross-legged and closed her paperback. "Do you think we have to cook in order to eat?"

Maddie would bet the answer to that was yes. Mason wasn't the kind of guy you took advantage of, and while she hadn't asked his policy on free lunches when they'd run into each other at the lookout yesterday, she could certainly venture a guess. While she stared, Mason started dicing mango with easy confidence. She was all thumbs when it came to knives. Mason… was not.

"He's going to make us work for it," she said with a petulant frown.

Ashley sighed. "You think he's a hard-ass about everything?"

"Probably." If she took her friend's words at face value, she had to admit that the man certainly had an amazing butt.

"Remember the drinks menu," Ashley said impishly. "You could take him for a test drive."

The *rumored* drinks menu, she reminded herself. The menu existed. She'd spent far too much time flipping through the twelve laminated pages of drinks with sexy names like *Leather and Lace* and *Kinky Sex.* The question, however, was whether those drink names were really not-so-covert code names for naughty sex acts that could be requested from the staff or other guests. Laney Parker had certainly made a good case for the menu being fact rather than fiction. She'd hooked up with the resort's super-sexy masseuse and, from her blushes, done some menu exploring with him. It was too bad the other woman had been unexpectedly called home when a new job had opened up for her at a local emergency room, because Maddie had questions. Like, could you really just point and pick? For some reason, the notion felt kind of slimy. "Do you really think Mason's available for *that*?"

Ashley shrugged. "Ask him."

"A guy who looks like that isn't available." Not in her universe and not with her dating bad luck.

Ashley ogled Mason. "Are you offering him to me?"

No. She really wasn't. "He's off-limits," she blurted, surprising herself. She hadn't decided yet if she was going for him, but she knew she didn't want to watch Ashley making a move on her chef.

"He's all yours," Ashley said, looking at her over the top of her sunglasses. "But you have to tell me what you're planning for him."

"He may not be interested," she warned.

"Oh, he's interested." Ashley grinned and, although they both knew she had no way of being certain about Mason's interest, Maddie appreciated the support.

Maddie didn't want to explain how many times she'd met a guy and gone after him, only to learn that *he* thought of *her* as the fun friend. At the last wedding she'd attended, the usher she'd been paired with had spent the evening reception hitting her up for the maid of honor's phone number. His patent disinterest in her own charms had rankled, too, because *she'd* thought they had good chemistry. Clearly, her dating radar was broken.

"Remember," she said lightly. "I'm always the bridesmaid and never the bride."

"How many times?"

It took a minute to do the math. "Thirteen. And gig number fourteen is coming up in a month. I have enough bridesmaid dresses in my closet to open my own bridal shop."

Ashley made a sympathetic face. "You think they'd notice if you recycled and wore one more than once?"

"They'd notice," she said with feeling. She'd dealt with more than one bridezilla.

Ashley nodded. "So. What's the plan?"

She didn't have one.

"Pick a drink," her friend advised. "Imagine the possibilities. I'll get you started. *Dirty Girl Scout. Sex on the Farm. Sexy Alligator.*"

"You made that one up."

"Right here on the menu." Ashley stabbed the plastic with her finger.

"Alligators aren't sexy," she protested. And sex on a farm didn't sound particularly exciting, either. She was more of a sex-on-a-yacht-with-a-billionaire type of gal.

Ashley shrugged unrepentantly. "Imagine Mason's face if you asked for *that*. You could get him to do anything."

They both turned to stare at him. Nope. Imagining that was even harder than finding the sexy in an alligator. Ashley wasn't deterred.

"*Pink Panties. Sex in the Driveway. Long Slow Screw Against the Wall.*" Ashley waved a hand. "Stop me when I get warm."

"That sounds so cheesy," she objected. But it also sounded fun. Her stomach hurt from laughing.

"Think of all the ways to improve your love life." Ashley smirked at her, as if finding an improved sex life was that simple.

Maddie stared at her margarita. No easy answer in the mango-flavored cocktail. Even though she was technically here on a working vacation, she'd been encouraged to sample everything the resort had to offer. So she could *better describe it for her blog followers.* She'd been more than happy to comply. A free week of R & R at an all-inclusive luxury villa? Sign her up. She could do whatever she wanted. Check out the beach. Go to lunch twice. Spend all her afternoons lazing in the sun or lying out at the spa.

Alone.

She hadn't considered the implications of being a party of one until her seaplane had been wheels down— did seaplanes even have wheels?—surrounded by happy, honeymooning, we're-having-fantastic-sex couples. Truthfully? She was lonely. Envious. Horny. As she watched other couples kissing and holding hands and generally getting started on happily-ever-after, she was feeling more than a little left out.

She clutched the mango margarita, fighting the urge to make a face. She had nothing to complain about. *Hello, free vacation?* It was just that she had kind of imagined that someday *she* would be the bride and that there would be a Mr. Maddie by her side to frolic on the island with her. Instead, she had another bridesmaid gig lined up for next month, and her lunchtime companion was another singleton she'd met on the seaplane.

Not that Ashley wasn't fantastic. She was.

A shadow fell over them. "Ladies," a familiar deep voice said. Mason stood over them, big and stern. *Oops.*

MADDIE KNEW HOW to follow orders. Sort of. And definitely in her own unique, impulsive way. Mason probably shouldn't read anything into Maddie's attendance of his cooking class, but she was trouble and he had a feeling they both knew it.

After he broke up her gossipfest with Ashley, she bounced up to the temporary cooking station he'd pointed her to as though he hadn't just interrupted a conversation about her dating life. Her bikini hugged her gorgeous curves and made his fingers itch to touch her, to smooth the fabric away and uncover bare skin. Her red hair was pulled up in a ponytail that brushed her shoulders with each jaunty step she took, and she had a pair of big white sunglasses pushed up on top of her head. Her cover-up was some kind of wrap thing with fringe on the sleeves that made him think of bedrooms. And getting naked. He thought a lot about getting naked when he was near Maddie.

She didn't seem to be mad at him about his startling her yesterday, which was a plus. On the other hand, she wasn't exactly paying all that much attention to him, either. Apparently, she wasn't harboring teacher fantasies.

Still, he couldn't help stealing glances at her and envisioning all the ways he could get to know her better. Make her feel better. She'd seemed…lonely. Even though she'd had her cute butt parked next to Ashley and had been laughing and talking up a storm like she always did, there was a hint of sadness in her eyes. Maybe it was just because she was literally here by herself and Fantasy Island didn't have a swinging singles scene. He'd never seen so many couples glued to each other outside a porn flick. He'd walked past the Jacuzzi the other night and his eyeballs still burned.

He lined his students up at the table, passed out mangoes, and then knives. Since he only had the four students, giving Ashley a wide berth was difficult, but he managed. Guests three and four were a honeymooning couple more interested in each other than mangoes. That was fine with him. Teaching crepe making was new to him, so the smaller the audience, the better. As soon as he barked *go*, Maddie obediently went to town on her mango, wielding her knife with more enthusiasm than skill. She attacked the fruit the same way she appeared to attack life—head-on.

She was beautiful, but that wasn't the reason for his attraction. Or, rather, it wasn't the sole reason. As hokey as it sounded, when she got close, he wanted to smile. To hold her in his arms and dance her around in a big old circle until she collapsed against him, dizzy and laughing. He wanted to laugh with her—and he'd felt that way since he first landed on the island and had set eyes on her.

She was someone special. And if there was an edge of desperation beneath her laughter, he wanted to know that side of her, too. She wasn't just the life of the party, even if that was what she wanted the world to believe. And he didn't think for one second that she was content with standing on the sidelines, watching wedding after wedding. So what *did* she want?

A piece of mango hit the pool deck. She cursed, and nearly amputated her finger, and he decided it was time for an intervention. Her fruit was a mangled mess and he'd sharpened the Wüsthofs himself that morning.

"Did the mango do something to piss you off?"

She stopped chopping with a sigh, pink tingeing her cheekbones. "At least you can still tell it's a mango, right?"

Only because he'd passed the fruit out himself. Otherwise he wouldn't have been able to identify the goopy yellow mass. Handling a knife was second nature for him. His Swiss Army knife had gotten him out of nearly as many jams as his combat knife. Reaching around her, he adjusted her grip. "Keep the bottom of the blade on the cutting board. Make sure the tip is up."

She brightened even as she impaled her knife on her cutting board. "I get points for effort, right?"

Her hair smelled good, like strawberries and coconut beneath the added bonus layer of mangoes. She also had mango juice on her fingers, her front and her cheek. He tried not to think about all the other places she could have self-decorated.

Focus. "Think squares."

"Squares." She sounded skeptical. He moved closer until his front was plastered up against her sweet butt. She inhaled, but didn't protest.

"First one big square, then four smaller squares, then sixteen."

"Math isn't my thing."

"Just dice."

He mentally consulted what he'd dubbed the boyfriend cheat sheet. He needed to compliment her in a meaningful way. Establish a sense of emotional intimacy. Honestly, he had no clue what that meant, although telling her that her hair smelled nice probably didn't count. A piece of flying mango hit him on the shoulder as he opened his mouth to praise her on her mad chopping skills.

Emphasis on *mad*.

"Oops," she said and grinned up at him. He knew a deliberate hit when he saw one. If she wanted to play dirty, he was happy to play with her.

"Can I take over?"

She dropped the knife—and leaned back against him.

"I'll take that as a yes," he said, and she blushed.

"Chopping's hard work. You can be my mango boy anytime," she said, surrendering the knife. If he was smart, he wouldn't read anything into it. Apparently, though, he'd checked his brain when he'd accepted her as his mission, because he could feel a small answering smile tugging at his mouth.

After he'd chopped her mango—and, Jesus, he wished that was a euphemism for something else—he moved down the table, checking on his other students. Ashley had her mango chopped into precise cubes. "Show-off," he muttered, and she stuck her tongue out at him. All good there. The honeymooning couple at the far end had progressed to feeding each other slices of fruit, and he resisted the urge to tell them to get a room. They had one. They just weren't using it.

Yet.

Fantasy Island made a guy think about sex about fifty times a minute. It didn't help that Maddie was covered in mango juice, making her his very own sweet sticky treat. Her crepe had achieved some strange mutant shape that defied the round shape of the pan. He didn't know what it was, but it certainly was no circle. It figured she'd make quirky crepes.

He peeled her crepe off the bottom of her pan and gave it a quick QA check. The top was raw and the bottom blackened. With a sigh, he substituted his crepe for hers.

She flashed him a dazzling smile. "Thank you. For the rescue," she added after a brief pause. He didn't know whether she meant yesterday on the hillside— or the mangoes.

"I still owe you makeup chocolate," he said gruffly.

Her head whipped around, her ponytail slapping him in the mouth. "You meant that?"

"You bet." He wiped a smudge of honey off the corner of her mouth. "I live to serve."

That much was true. His family served. It was their tradition and he was proud to continue it. He'd do what he could do, push to be the best that he could be. Sure, he'd been the first to do it for Uncle Sam rather than Fish & Game or the Forest Service, but he figured service was like Christmas presents. It came in different sizes and shapes and sometimes you had no idea what you were getting, but it was all good. His dad had been a hotshot firefighter. His uncles were firefighters, too. He'd simply picked a different kind of fire, the kind that came with bad guys and bullets…and Maddie. Being her bodyguard detail was a whole different challenge.

She stared at him, evaluating something he couldn't see. "Tomorrow?"

"It's a date."

"Like a *date* date?" Was that a hint of uncertainty in her eyes? He couldn't tell, but that was nothing new. He wasn't the kind of guy who dated much and being an active-duty SEAL made relationships near impossible. He never knew when he would be called up or for how long, which made any kind of connection or friendship outside his team difficult.

"Makeup chocolate," he repeated, skirting the whole thorny issue of their relationship potential.

She gave him another assessing look and then grinned. "Okay. Sounds like fun, so why the *hell* not?"

He, on the other hand, could think of multiple reasons. He was staring down thirty—from the wrong side of the decade. Although he still had all his working parts, he was banged up something fierce. His knees were good; his trigger finger steady. In short, he was a fixer-upper project and she was no carpenter.

"Give me a time, big guy," she said, leaning in and patting his chest. "So I can prepare properly."

Yeah. He was definitely out of his league here. Maddie was a dating guru, unlike his sorry self. At the very least, his instant erection was ironclad proof that she'd mastered the fine art of flirting.

"Eight o'clock," he muttered and beat a strategic retreat.

4

I've got a breakfast date this morning with Mr. Fantasy Fodder (and I should sign off because, yep, it's three in the morning and the purple shadows under my eyes are *not* a sexy look). I'll report back on whether or not FF lives up to the promise of his mighty fine butt! I'm taking bets on which approach I should take:

A) Point him in the direction of the Cheerios in my kitchen. They're heart healthy—and probably not too stale.

B) Hop out of bed and throw together a quick Sunday brunch for two because the way to his heart is either through his stomach or his libido—and I'm the kind of gal who likes to have all the bases covered.

C) Offer to split the last package of Pop-Tarts with him. Naked. In bed.

—MADDIE, Kiss and Tulle

STEP ONE IN becoming the perfect boyfriend? Cook Maddie a romantic breakfast and make her feel butterflies when she looked at him. No pressure. Since Maddie had agreed to a chocolate-chip pancake date, Mason had breakfast covered. He'd cook her a short stack, suss out her electronics and wipe any data that needed wiping. Easy-peasy and a guaranteed success, according to the magazine article Mason had checked out. *Keep the doubts to yourself.*

She looked like the girl next door, the queen of diamond rings, tulle and happily-ever-afters. So not his style. But until SEAL Team Sigma had ruled out the possibility of finding Santiago Marcos on the island, Mason would stick by her side. That was the *only* reason he was knocking on her door this morning, he told himself. Security reasons…not personal pursuits. SEALs shipped out. He'd known a few married men in the teams, but he wasn't going to be a part-time husband, lover, father. His Mrs. was the military.

Maddie's villa was the first in a row of picture-perfect bungalows dotting a white sand beach. He knew from the team's orientation that she'd have a small kitchen because apparently some of the island's guests liked to throw intimate dinner parties or have a private chef come in to whip up dinner. It was a different world from the loud, noisy family culinary sessions he'd grown up with. Today though, the secluded-elegance crap worked for him. Cooking in the resort's immaculate industrial kitchen wouldn't have let him get close to Maddie.

Although he had a staff passkey, he knocked. And then waited. Double-checked the bungalow number to make sure he was in the right place. Waited some more while he considered the possibility that there had already been a security breach and Santiago had gotten to Maddie. His gut tightened. There were no visible signs of forcible entry, and it was more likely she'd simply overslept. At this rate, she'd be eating breakfast for lunch. The third time he knocked, he finally heard footsteps.

When Maddie eventually cracked the door and peered out, he stared back because he couldn't help himself. She was wearing a pink tank top and cotton sleep shorts that barely skimmed the top of her curvy thighs. Her hair was piled on top of her head in a death-defying, messy bun. Red strands escaped around her face, already curling in the island's humidity.

"The sun's not up yet," she mumbled, patting the mountain of curls into some semblance of order.

It was eight o'clock. And the only thing not up yet was Maddie. He was also fairly certain her eyes were shut, even if her mouth was open. She was a rumpled, adorable mess and she looked as if she'd rolled right out of bed—so, naturally, he wanted to roll her right back in.

"Pancakes." He held up his box of ingredients.

"Right." She leaned against the door as if she planned on going back to sleep right there. Time for a new strategy. He set the box down on the ground, reached in and gently lifted her out of the way so he could open the door. Then he nudged the box inside with his foot, stepped in and closed the door behind him.

"Wow." She blinked at him as if he'd managed to surprise him. He only hoped it was in a good way. "Way to make a girl feel good about her weight."

He ran his eyes over her. She looked fantastic. Given his overabundance of sisters, however, he knew better than to touch that particular statement. There was absolutely, positively no crowd-pleasing answer. Instead, he gave her a slow smile. The corners of her mouth turned up in response.

"You're not a morning person." He picked up his box.

"I'm at my best at night." She turned and padded away, waving a hand toward the kitchen. "Make yourself at home."

Her sleep shorts were riding up her gorgeous ass. He wanted to squeeze and cup, nip that sweet, soft curve. And she wanted breakfast. He kicked off his shoes at the door and did a quick check of the room. Bingo. She'd left her laptop in its case on the coffee table. Snagging it, he stepped back to the door, opened it and signaled. Levi appeared on the path, pushing a housekeeping cart.

Thirty seconds elapsed. Levi passed him a stack of towels and a laptop; Mason handed over Maddie's laptop and performed a little case switcheroo. "Time?"

"I'm making breakfast. You should have at least an hour."

"Aww…how domestic." Levi tucked Maddie's laptop into the housekeeping cart, just hotel staff delivering towels. "I'll have this back in twenty, unless our girl actually practices password security. In which case, give me thirty."

"Laptop goes on the coffee table facing the front door. Walk it in, go straight. You can't miss it."

"Got it." Levi nodded and stepped off the porch. Mason put the decoy laptop back on the coffee table and made for the kitchen. Coffee was his next priority. Black for him. Since she seemed to like sweet stuff, he laced hers with dulce de leche and then added chocolate sprinkles and whipped cream.

When she padded back into the kitchen five minutes later, he smelled toothpaste, but she hadn't bothered to get dressed. Instead, she'd tossed a kimono over her pajamas. Cheerful, loud red flowers on something that was sheer and turquoise and... Jesus. He could see her sun-kissed skin through the fabric.

Remember the magazine strategy.

Ogling her in her own kitchen wasn't endearing. It was creepy. Unfortunately, the peekaboo glimpses of her delectable curves drove the magazine quiz straight out of his head. Ten steps to success. It was a nice plan. Simple. Easy to implement. Instead of working on "forging an intimate connection," however, he nearly swallowed his tongue at the little whimper of pleasure she made when she took her first sip of coffee.

"God. That's so good." Her fingers stroked the side of the coffee mug. Which was white ceramic and not his dick, so the bolt of heat that shot straight to his groin was completely unexplainable. She didn't stop the tiny orgasmic sounds as she drained his coffee and, who knew—his dick could, in fact, get harder.

He stepped closer to the stove. Pancakes, not sex. He needed to remember the mission. Which was *not* "get Mason laid," no matter what certain iron-like parts of his body suggested.

He'd mixed the batter before coming, so it shouldn't take more than ten minutes to make her breakfast. He turned on the stove, which heated up far more slowly than he had. He brushed a pan with butter, turned to grab the batter and slammed into her. *So not the romantic plan.* Involuntarily, his hands shot straight to her hips to steady her and his fingers brushed the top of her ass in an all-around, worst-ever Whiskey Tango Foxtrot.

"Whoops," she said, flushing. She didn't take a step backward, though. He couldn't help but notice that. No, she stayed plastered thigh to thigh and front to front with him. And she had a spectacular front.

"You okay?" No one got the drop on him, but this one woman was apparently the exception.

"Can I help?" Avoiding his eyes, she reached around him and started rummaging through his box. Any semblance of order vanished at approximately the same speed her shorts rode up her curvy ass. The kimono did nothing to shield it from his gaze, and, boy, was he enjoying looking. That had to be why he didn't mind the mess. That, and the fact that Maddie could break him down faster than he could an M4.

Without waiting for his answer—which was, he realized, typical—she pulled herself up on the counter, parked her sweet butt next to his gear and crossed her legs. She waved a spatula she'd found in the box.

"What a girl could do with this," she said, slapping the plastic against her palm. His brain stuttered to a halt while his body went into autopilot pouring batter onto the griddle. Had she really gone there?

She grinned and held out the spatula. When he took it, her fingers slid over his. Lingered. She was definitely trouble.

"Is that a dare?" Breakfast. Compliments. Long walks on the beach. A few slow, wet kisses. And then, according to the magazine master plan, he got to have sex with her. Except that he had to substitute screwing with her electronics for sleeping with Maddie, he reminded himself. Clearly, he had his priorities skewed and should have focused on bringing the kink.

Equally clearly, she planned on skipping straight to the climax, so to speak. Or she was just messing with him. Either seemed like a possibility. The wicked gleam in her eyes had him voting for option B.

"Do you want it to be?" She returned her attention to the contents of the box. Unfortunately for her curiosity, he'd left the BDSM arsenal in the hotel gift shop.

"You don't want to play games with me, sweetheart."

She shrugged. "Don't be so sure of that."

"I always win." Even before BUD/S training, he'd learned the value of winning. Older sisters were merciless when triumphant.

"Don't be so sure of that, either." She grinned cheekily at him. "Your pancakes are bubbling. Even I know that means it's time to flip."

Shit. He rescued the pancakes, turning them over and adding the chocolate chips, before setting out a plate.

She watched him work, swinging a bare foot. She pouted. "You're not eating with me? Because it's just wrong to ignore chocolate chips."

Silently he added a second plate to the counter. Guess he could be tempted after all.

MAYBE SHE COULD blame Fantasy Island. Maybe the place simply had sex in the air, like perfume at the mall. Or maybe Maddie was just lonely. That last option wasn't her favorite, but she had to admit the possibility. Her recent dating history consisted of long stretches of drought peppered with spectacular failures. Since working from home on her blog ruled out a workplace romance, she'd had to rely on the guys she met at weekend weddings. While she found a guy in a tux as hot as the next woman did, she'd also discovered that a tux was a version of dating wallpaper. The sexy suit covered up a wealth of issues. She didn't need another DIY fixer-upper man.

Been there, done that.

A year ago, she'd naively thought her then boyfriend had been on the proposal train. Unfortunately, the special dinner she'd anticipated all week had turned out to be the breakup dinner. He'd picked up the check, though, after explaining that he'd accepted a work transfer to the other side of the country—and that he thought they should take a break while he "got settled." She'd ordered both the lobster and the Kir Royal cocktail. Three times. The rest of the night had been a mindless blur, although she'd apparently drunk texted her sisters the sorry details of her sex life. Twelve months later, she still hadn't lived those texts down.

Hot vacation sex with Mason might seem like the best of ideas, but it could all too easily end like her last relationship. Being the punch line in a bad joke wasn't funny. At all. She had an adjective for every finger on her hand for wrestling Mason into bed: *risky, impulsive* and...*tingly.* While she'd enjoyed the casual post-wedding hookup, Mason was dangerous to her peace of mind. Once might not be enough with him.

Maybe it was all the weddings. Thirteen of them in eighteen months. Once upon a time, weddings had been her favorite way to spend a Saturday, but she was tired of standing on the sidelines. Tired of watching other people hook up and live out their fantasies. She didn't need a groom of her own, but a man? Temporarily? That worked for her. Where was the harm in borrowing Mason for the rest of her vacation? The hunk definitely brought out her inner tease.

Bad Maddie.

He was big and built, powerful shoulders flexing beneath his white T-shirt. She had no idea how he stayed so pristine in the kitchen. There wasn't a smear of flour or chocolate on him anywhere she could see. It was like her own personal challenge to see if she could crack his stoic surface and mess him up. Only in the best possible ways, she thought virtuously. Nothing mean or petty. Just…sexy.

God, was he ever sexy.

And that was *before* he said the magic words. "Strawberries or whipped cream?" The smile quirking the corner of his mouth was downright naughty. "Or both?"

"You have to ask?" Because, seriously, was there more than one possible answer?

"A vote for both." With a flourish, he spread strawberries over the topmost pancakes and followed with whipped cream, and not the kind from the aerosol bottle. Nope. He had a fancy stainless-steel number that promised all sorts of dairy goodness. There was definitely something to be said for a man who cooked. He picked up the two plates and nodded his head toward the small table. "Sit down."

Fresh whipped cream was a motivator. She hopped off the counter and sat at the table.

He wasn't much of a talker. He didn't open up and tell her all about himself, or even share the usual dating details like favorite movies, favorite songs or favorite sexual positions. Instead, he sat there and listened.

She told herself that wasn't a turn-on, but really…yeah. It was.

"What made you decide to blog about weddings?"

"I was laid off. I knew how to type." She wiggled her French-manicured fingers at him. "And I had a stack of wedding invitations as high as Bill Mountain."

"A fresh start." He nodded grimly, as if he understood, although she had to wonder what he'd ever failed at. He seemed pretty darn perfect to her.

She and failure, on the other hand, were BFFs. She'd been an executive assistant before the software start-up folded. No Silicon Valley billionaire had crossed her path, although she'd had a few conference room fantasies to go with a social life that consisted of online dating, dating apps and friends of friends. She gave good first dates, but guys didn't call back. Or email back, text back or IM her back, and it was partly her fault. She knew what she wanted in a man and she knew she had things to offer. He'd be honest and reliable and, when she was around him, she'd feel safe enough to be herself. He'd like her first, and then he'd love her. In exchange for all of himself, she'd offer up all she had. She definitely wouldn't have sex *just because* or to cross the next step off in some dating checklist. But even if she was looking for Mr. Right, she'd also settle for an attractive Mr. Right Now as long as he came with an orgasm for two.

"Bills are an excellent motivator," she admitted softly.

He laughed. "Yeah. Electricity and running water are kind of addictive."

She'd marked the date on her calendar when she'd earned enough from affiliate marketing to pay her rent.

Forget celebrating dating anniversaries—because *that* had been a day to remember.

"Why weddings?" he continued. "Other than a pressing need to keep the lights on."

"You don't think I'm a personal expert?"

He gave her another lazy grin. "Are you admitting to being a serial bride?"

"I was a bona fide expert. I'd been to a dozen in five months because my college friends paired off like randy rabbits. I'd also worn out my copy of *Wedding Crashers* and thought, 'I could do that.' One big party with free food and bad dresses, right? Then I found out that I actually like weddings. I like the food, the flowers, the really bad and over-the-top dresses. And, yes, I like the look the groom gets on his face when he sees his bride walking up the aisle toward him." She paused. "Does that scare you?"

He finished his last pancake and stole a bite of hers. "Not particularly. Is this where your other dates run screaming for the exit?"

"Honestly? Yeah." She sighed. Blogging about weddings was like having the best-ever paper-dolls set, where she could try on all the clothes and the locations for herself, but without committing. Guys, however, seemed to assume she had to score a ring of her own ASAP. At the very least, they expected an endless series of boring Saturdays dressed up in a tuxedo. And while she wanted to find The One and get hitched, it didn't have to happen this week, this month or even this year. Just…sometime. Sometime would be good.

"Who knew?" He'd eaten with neat efficiency, dividing each pancake into even sections. Finished, he lined up his knife and fork on the edge of the plate with military precision.

She, on the other hand, had only a passing familiarity with the word *neat*. It had zero practical applications to her everyday life. She pointed a fork at him. "Finish your thought."

"That someone could make a living writing about weddings on the internet."

"Not a good living," she muttered. "This Fantasy Island gig is my shot at serious advertising revenue. If I do a good job here, other clients should follow. Hopefully before the electric company turns off my power."

He laughed. "So you're the Pied Piper of the blogosphere."

"Except the Pied Paper was kind of creepy—and he had thousands of rats following him." She, on the other hand, had an entourage of one. "You're a good listener." Whoops. The words had come out more accusation than not.

He shrugged. "I have sisters."

And she'd bet they worshipped him. The twinkle in his eyes said the feeling was mutual. "How many?"

"Too many?" A smile tugged at his gorgeous mouth as he relaxed, his arms stretched out over the back of the bench. His bare feet brushed against hers. He was in her space.

And she liked it.

"Four," he continued. "I have four sisters. A mother. Three aunties and three female cousins. I get plenty of practice listening."

She could just imagine. "No wonder you're not much of a talker."

"Pick a topic."

She eyed him suspiciously. "You're willing to make a blanket commitment to talking about anything?"

"You're right. That could get me in trouble." He pushed to his feet. Oh, yum. All smooth male power. "I should clean up."

No. He should get really, really dirty.

"I have a few ideas." Reaching out, she hooked a finger in the hem of his T-shirt.

"Of where to start?" Now he looked amused. Or maybe that was the strawberry smear she'd just deposited on his shirt. Switching hands, she stuck her finger in her mouth and sucked it clean. He made a hoarse sound as if he felt the pull of her mouth in interesting places.

Definitely not interested in letting go. "Are you cursing?"

"I'm cleaning," he said firmly, grabbing her plate as if she didn't have a stranglehold on his shirt.

She tugged a little harder. *Come closer.* "You need one of those maid's aprons."

"You see me in white-and-black frills? Besides, I think that might count as sexual harassment." He set the plates down and freed his shirt. She couldn't help but notice, however, that he didn't step back.

"Are you complaining?" Because if he was, she could take the hint.

He shook his head, gave her a mock-stern look. "I should."

"You have whipped cream on your mouth." Since he was so conveniently close…she tucked her fingers in the waistband of his pants and pulled. No need for words—his new position put him almost on eye level with her.

"Bossy," he said with another one of his slow, sexy smiles. And then, "Prove it."

She loved a good dare.

"Right here." She scooped up whipped cream from her plate and pressed a fingertip against the corner of his mouth. "I'll help you with it."

Mason's eyes darkened and he slammed his hands down on either side of her legs, leaning in. His shoulders pressed her thighs wide and she fought the urge to drape them over his shoulders and tell him to dive on in, but she didn't want to put him off. She knew what she liked and she wasn't afraid to ask for it, but some guys were scared off by that. It was their loss, but if Mason was a card-carrying member of the Men With Small Penises Club, their pancake-eating fun would be over.

On the other hand...she had Fantasy Island's hunkiest guy almost on his knees in front of her. How could she not take advantage of that? Every romantic chick flick she'd seen flashed through her head, followed by more than one scene from her favorite romance novel. She really shouldn't tease him, but her body ignored the caution and leaned closer and closer until she ran the risk of falling off the chair and all she could see was Mason. God, he was gorgeous.

And he was kissing distance away, his chiseled lips mere inches from hers.

Since her mouth was so close to his, she brushed her lips against the corner of his mouth. He inhaled. Exhaled something that might have been her name. *Yes, please*, her hormones sang and she licked him, bracing her hands against his hard, warm shoulders just so she wouldn't topple him to the floor. He tasted sweet, a sweet that was deceptive because, darn it, there was absolutely, positively nothing sweet about Mason. He was 100 percent trouble, even kneeling before her.

"Problem solved," she whispered and kissed him.

5

"YOU'RE ASKING FOR TROUBLE." The gruff words came out of Mason's mouth uninvited. He didn't know why he was complaining. He wasn't opposed to kissing. In fact, completing his mission practically called for it, what with the whole "make her feel butterflies" plan. This was also the part where he kept her busy with his mouth and won her trust, so he had an ironclad reason for sticking by her side. Plus, over her shoulder, he could see the front door open silently as Levi slid inside and made for the coffee table to swap the laptops.

She smiled down at him. Not a teasing grin, but a big, wide smile that lit up her pretty face and made him want to smile right back. It was hard not to get pulled into Maddie's orbit. She was Planet Sexy to his Moon of... Christ. He didn't know. He sucked at metaphors. Or whatever.

She ran her finger over his bottom lip and heat streaked through him, almost driving all nonsexual thoughts out of his head. "I prefer to think of it as creative rule bending."

Maddie was the best kind of trouble, her fingers

skimming over his mouth, leaving whipped cream and destruction in her wake. How the hell was he supposed to stick to the plan now? He sucked her finger into his mouth, exploring her skin with his tongue. When he bit gently, she moaned. And smiled again. He had a bad feeling she'd let him do far more than simply kiss her. Was he that much of a jackass that he'd seduce her in the name of his mission?

"What's the punishment for getting in trouble?" Blissfully unaware of his inner dilemma or the SEAL leaving her living room with a quick flash of the finger, she caught his lower lip between her teeth and bit right back. Jesus. She wasn't shy at all. A bright, hot flare of pleasure shot straight from his mouth to his dick. He didn't know if that had been her intention, but damn, she was good. And…screw the mission. *Poor choice of words.* He put his hands on her thighs and slid his palms up over smooth, silky skin. Her barely there shorts were no barrier, more like a teasing end goal. He could keep touching her, have his fingers beneath the cotton in seconds, and then… She gave a purr of approval.

"Go on a date with me." The words shot out of his mouth before he could bite them back. He wanted it all, right now.

She nibbled on her lower lip, clearly thinking about his offer. And…so much for restraint or sticking to the plan. The plan had been a terrible idea. The worst ever. Kissing her, on the other hand, was the best. He slanted his lips over hers and she gave a sigh of pleasure, melting into him.

Her new position pulled her off balance and he liked that, too. Damn it. She was half perched on her chair and he was crouched before her. Her nails dug into his shoulder as she reached for him.

"I like a man on his knees."

She clearly thought she had the upper hand, but he was happy to prove her wrong. He reached, too, cupping her neck with his hand and bringing her face down to his. He gave her three seconds to decide whether or not she wanted this and to fall back, but all she did was exhale softly, her gaze fixed on his mouth. Definitely a yes in his book. Since she apparently liked her kisses sweet, and whatever she liked was more than fine by him, he swiped a finger of whipped cream from his plate and painted the stuff over her mouth.

"Oh." She sounded pleased, her lashes fluttering shut in delicate submission.

Slowly, he closed the distance between them, spinning out the moment because she was so goddamned pretty, brushing his lips over hers again, when she finally remembered to breathe and exhaled. Her mouth was slick and sugar sweet, a wicked invitation to explore. Unable to resist, he licked her bottom lip, drinking in her husky moan. The sultry little sound cut off, as if she wasn't so sure about letting go for him. He'd just have to convince her. He made a list of the places he could coat her with whipped cream, starting with her lovely breasts and moving south.

He pressed his mouth against hers and her lips parted. A little more pressure and he was in, his tongue tangling with hers. Deeper, hotter. He tasted the sugary bite of the cream and something else that was all Maddie. She was a bright, hot flavor, like sunshine and happiness, and he had absolutely no basis for comparison. He was no kissing virgin, but Maddie was

someone special. He recognized that truth even as he
stroked his tongue into her mouth, taking more. She
was addictive, too.

With a whimper of encouragement, she met him,
giving as good as she got, and, dear God, he was a
lucky man. The morning was perfect. She was as sweet
as she tasted, although he already knew she had a side
of sass and tart and would kick his ass if she ever found
out about the undercover SEAL mission. He'd deserve
it, too, but right now he had Maddie in his arms and
no way he was giving that up. He might have offered
pancakes under false pretenses, but there was nothing
fake about their kiss.

When he broke away, her lips clung to his as if she
wasn't done with him yet. Thank God. He wasn't done
with her, not by a long shot.

"You got an answer for me, sugar?" Yes worked for
him. *Tonight* was even better.

Her lashes drifted up slowly, as if she was lost somewhere pleasurable, in another world. He found that in-
credibly intoxicating. He'd touch her for hours, love on
her every way possible. He rubbed a trace of cream he'd
missed with his thumb, relishing the way she turned
into the little caress.

"Remind me of the question." She sounded dazed
and content. Damned if he didn't like that, too.

"I'd like to see you again," he said gruffly. He was
no Mr. Suave, but he meant every word. Hell, it was
the understatement of the year. He more than *liked*. He
needed. He…was in over his head.

"YOU WANT ME to go out with you?" It was official.
Kisses could make a gal stupid and her brain had

stopped working somewhere about half a kiss ago. Maybe that had something to do with the man on his knees before her, his thumbs stroking a naughty pattern over the sensitive skin of her inner thighs. *So good.* She was on fire for him, needing and achy in ways she hadn't felt for months. Years. He lifted her hand to his mouth, gently sucking the last bit of whipped cream from her finger. *Oh.* His lips moved, repeating something, but English wasn't on her radar right now.

"On a date," he said, his mouth brushing over hers again.

Whatever he wanted, a million times yes, as long as it meant more kisses *now*. When she didn't answer right away, he continued, "I've decided that you said yes. Or at least 'I'll think about it' or 'maybe.' Because the way you kissed me back? That wasn't a 'when hell freezes over and thaws out again.'" He dropped a quick kiss on her lips and stood up.

"Um. Wait. You're leaving?" Because that definitely hadn't been part of her fantasy when she'd put herself out there. She'd moved full steam ahead to bedroom things. And orgasm things. She might not be good at long-term relationships and her dating skills were a bit rusty, but her bedroom skills? Rocked.

Plus, as soon as she got back from Fantasy Island, she had her fourteenth wedding of the year to attend and she was once again going solo, so she deserved a Mason-size treat right now. She could totally do sex.

With this man.

It was true that around him she felt like the sexiest woman in the world. But despite the heated sensations coursing through her body, he made her feel something else, too. Something…warm. And entirely unfamiliar. He needed to stay so she could figure it all out.

"Afraid so, sweetheart."

"But what if I'm not done kissing you?"

"More kisses could be arranged." The man had an impressive serious face. Still, how hard could it be to talk him into more kissing? He was a guy. He was biologically hardwired to put out.

She stared up at him for a moment before bolting to her feet. Staying where she was put him in a serious power position. "How about now?"

He started across the room, clearly not on board with the take-Mason-to-bed plan, and suddenly she didn't feel so sexy anymore. The fun was gone and what she felt was—

Disappointment.

Instead of making for the door, however, he grabbed her phone from its precarious resting spot beside her bag.

"I'm going to give you my number," he said. "Unlock your phone for me."

The "tell, don't ask" approach shouldn't have been such a turn-on, but she nodded her head and tapped in the passcode to her phone when he handed it to her. Really, he was every bit as pushy as she was. He just did it more nicely. *Sucker*, a little voice in her head catcalled. *Sexual drought*, other parts of her chanted right back.

He gave her a small, crooked smile that made her melt in all the best places. Then he typed in a number and handed her phone back to her. "Call me."

What was wrong with right now?

"I have to go to work," he continued, as if he'd read her mind.

Which was scary. Her head thought up things she had positively no intention of sharing with anyone, even if the "anyone" in question was six feet plus of masculine hotness. Of course, if she wanted to share any of those fantasies with him, she was going to have to call him after all, because he hotfooted it out her door as if his mighty fine ass was on fire.

USUALLY MASON LOVED his job, but the slow pace of this particular mission made him itch. Fast rope in, M4 at the ready, clear the site, secure the target and extract. That was his favorite mode. Instead, he was stuck on an island holding daily meetings as if he'd taken up residence in the corner office of a skyscraper.

It took almost twenty minutes to reach the camp. For a small private island, the place had a surprising amount of jungle. He eased a vine out of his way and moved past palm trees, palm trees and more palm trees. Fantasy Island also had a large selection of tropical plants, too many bugs and howler monkeys that chattered more than his sisters. Good times. When he finally stepped into the clearing, he found Levi leaned back against a palm tree, disassembling a M4—with the business end of a second gun trained on Mason's heart. The man wasn't their weapons expert for nothing. Sam, the team medic, crouched beside him. It was always good to have someone to pass out the Band-Aids.

"You might want to ring the doorbell and let a guy know you're coming," Levi drawled.

If Levi wanted a fight, Mason was more than happy to give him one. After all, *he* hadn't been trying to chat up a perfectly nice woman so he could rummage through her stuff. He slapped the magazine article against the other man's chest. "Being the perfect boyfriend was a spectacularly bad idea."

He didn't do *boyfriend*. Which, apparently, was just fine with Maddie. Maybe it was all the women in his life already, but when a guy had as many sisters and female cousins as he did, it was hard to *not* imagine how he'd feel if that was his sister and some guy was coming on to her under false pretenses. Maddie was cute and funny, and he'd run out of her villa before he gave in to temptation. Taking advantage of what she was offering was wrong. Really, really wrong and ten flavors of tempting. *Damn it*.

Levi flipped him the bird. "Implementation issues?"

"I implemented just fine." Including the part where he'd passed off a burner phone as his personal phone number. That was definitely a new low there.

"Uh-huh." Levi slotted the magazine into the stock and sighted down the barrel. "Then, why are you bitching?"

"She's off-limits."

"Morals. Nice. I'll see you with this—she's a nosy photographer who does not have a cache of incriminating photographs parked on her hardware, although she may be the only person on the island who can identify the brother of a notorious drug dealer." Levi didn't look up from his weapon. "Our objective was to confirm the existence or nonexistence of said cache and take appropriate follow-up action, while simultaneously preventing Santiago from taking her out. We're halfway to our goal, FYI."

Nicely put. "Her laptop was clean?"

Levi shrugged. "Except for copies of the time-lapse

photos we already know about. Ashley installed a program to reroute all her outbound internet through the CIA. She'll think she has crappy vacation internet, we'll look at her stuff before she posts and everyone lives happily ever after unless it turns out that Santiago *is* on the island."

"I'll stick to her like white on rice. If I'm not with her, one of you has eyes on her. Do we have an update on Santiago's whereabouts?" Comfort-wise, sitting here beat the hell out of waiting in a foxhole, swimming in sand or shit, but it was boring. The most fun he'd had was his fake date with Maddie yesterday, but he wasn't the guy she thought he was, and he knew she wouldn't understand the reasons for his deception. His next date needed to be with a jumpmaster and the open door of a helo—not with a gorgeous redhead.

"You want to fast rope out of here in the middle of the night?" Levi laughed, amused. "Subtle."

Ashley pointed to the satellite radio. "If we're done with the social chitchat, I've got Gray. He's still stateside, but he's got an update for us on Remy and new intel on Santiago."

A few minutes later, wondering if he hadn't been overly hasty when he'd wished for action, Mason listened as Gray laid out the details. Remy was headed stateside for more surgery and what looked to be months of recovery, although his doctors were "cautiously optimistic" he'd make a full recovery. Remy was stubborn, driven and a SEAL. Mason knew who he was betting on.

The new mission plan was equally optimistic. The team would insert by helo, meet up with the recon team and take up positions around the brothers' compound.

From the looks of the satellite photos, infiltrating would be a bitch. Santiago Marcos's secret hideaway backed onto some prime mountain real estate a hundred miles away on the Belizean mainland. What wasn't cliff-side was surrounded by thick jungle. His decorating scheme also appeared to feature concrete walls, barbed wire and a small army of bodyguards. Since it still wasn't clear if Santiago was home or not, they'd pay a house call and confirm for themselves.

"Meet Santiago Marcos." Ashley tapped the tablet, displaying a photograph of a fortysomething Hispanic male. "Two years younger than Diego Marcos. Five feet eight inches tall, brown hair, charcoal-brown eyes and no distinguishing marks other than a tattoo on his right biceps. Nice-looking dude."

"You looking to get laid?"

Ashley glared at Levi as Gray's voice came over the radio. "The FBI just got an indictment handed down in federal court, accusing him of drug trafficking and money laundering. We're cleared to bring him into US custody."

Levi sighed. "Is our guy a jogger? Do we think he's planning on taking a walk outside his place to check his tomato plants? Or do we get to do more than wander by and tackle him?"

Their actions at the objective were straightforward. Fly under the radar into the surrounding jungle and then infiltrate closer. Demolitions experts on the other team would blow a new front door in the compound walls, they'd storm in and then search the place from the bottom up. If they found Santiago in residence, they'd transport him to the extraction point from where it was a quick ride to US jurisdiction and a court date.

After they'd gone over what was required from each member of the team and the weapons they'd bring to the party, Mason only had one question.

"What are our rules of engagement?" Shooting the guy on sight would be good.

Gray issued a clear negative. "ROE says we can shoot only if Santiago offers provocation. In the meantime, you continue to patrol Fantasy Island and make sure no one shows up uninvited."

"Roger that." Maddie would never be alone. "Timeline?"

"We move in four nights," Gray said. "That gives us time to search Fantasy Island for Santiago while the recon team tries to verify that he really is holed up inside the compound."

They switched to discussing backup plans. Per standard operating protocol, they covered every what-if. Gray would rejoin them when they were on the Belize mainland, but until then Mason would lock down Fantasy Island. Nothing and no one got to Maddie on his watch.

Levi punched him in the arm. "We having fun yet?"

There was only one possible answer. "Hooyah."

6

Best first date ever! Guys, take note. Instead of doing the dinner-and-drinks thing (and did I mention that Fantasy Island has a very, very sexy cocktail menu?), Mr. Fantasy Fodder came by my villa super early in the morning (which wasn't so sexy—I had a serious case of bedhead) and made little old me chocolate-chip pancakes. Added bonus? Strawberries and whipped cream! Since FF was being a little standoffish (translation: insisted on keeping his hands to himself and being the perfect gentleman), I had to take offensive action, and all that whipped cream came in handy. Somehow, he ended up with a whipped cream mustache, and of course, I had to kiss it off. I'm sure he appreciated my efforts because he promptly asked me out on a date. I'm not sure where this is headed, ladies, but this is shaping up to be The Best Business Trip Ever. I'll report back soon!

—MADDIE, Kiss and Tulle

MASON SEEMED LIKE a genuinely nice guy with a rocking body. Maddie had dated her share of fun men, but she had a bad feeling that Mason was in a league of his own. The League of Supersweet Keeper Guys. If she was being honest, her area of expertise was first dates. She'd had plenty of them after all. It was making it to the second, third and fourth dates that posed a challenge. Plus, a long-term relationship was rarer than the dodo bird in her universe. Mason made her think that she had herself a bird sighting.

Besides, when had she ever held back? Mason, aka Mr. Fantasy Fodder, tempted her, so why not treat herself to a little taste of him? She was on a workcation and he was here. She saw him daily—in fact, now that she thought about it, pretty much every time she turned around—and her blog readers loved the guy. When she posted about him, her website traffic soared. Her readers had been begging for pictures, so she'd decided to tease them. She'd snapped a photo of Mason when he wasn't looking. Despite being fully dressed, he'd looked downright yummy. She'd also grabbed some extreme close-ups of the man's butt, front and every other fine attribute she could point her camera lens at. She was posting one piece a day so her readers could build their own island hottie.

She thunked her head on the bar. Okay. She had it bad for Mason, and not just because she lusted after his parts. Nope. She wanted the whole man. The warm look he got in his eyes when she said something particularly ridiculous, the killer grin he trained on her when she got him smiling, the big heart he hid just north of his six-pack abs…

"Writing not going well?" Ashley slid onto the bar stool next to her. "Nice shirt."

The writing was fine. It was her dating life that was

having a crisis. She'd picked out today's outfit to take her mind off Mason and the desirability of wearing no clothes at all. The result was a white bikini with a bandage top that crisscrossed her boobs and exposed her belly button. Just in case he didn't receive the "I'm so sexy" message—because clearly he wasn't getting *something*—she'd wrapped herself up in a slinky and sheer-as-hell sarong and slipped on high-heeled espadrilles. As long as she didn't have to win a footrace across the beach, she was all set. Pretty clothes were like armor. Most people didn't bother to look past them.

Compliment dispensed, Ashley pointed at Maddie's laptop. "What's the topic for today?"

"I'm brainstorming blog topics." No way she'd admit that her Mason crush was currently fueling her blog's soaring popularity.

Ashley shrugged. "Why not write about the cocktail menu? The *secret* one," she emphasized, flicking the menu disparagingly.

"Then, it wouldn't be a secret."

"I bet lots more people would visit the resort," she pointed out, nudging her sunglasses into place.

Maddie kind of liked the idea of a secret menu. Or possibly, she didn't want to share Mason with anyone else. Not that she had him, but it wasn't for lack of trying. She had no idea how anyone could be so darn perfect and yet maintain so much distance at the same time. He'd had his tongue in her mouth, for crying out loud. That was practically a dating commitment right there.

"You could try it." Ashley flashed a cajoling smile. "Just for your readers' benefit."

"You're a bad influence…but I'll think about it. Okay?"

Ashley shrugged. "Have it your way."

Sighing, Maddie tapped a key. Pressed it again. And then again. Shoot. Her computer was sluggish today, operating on island time. Since there wasn't a Genius Bar within a hundred miles of her, she really needed her hardware to behave.

Ashley's eyes followed her finger. "Problems?"

She banged the key again. Again—nothing. "My computer is acting funky."

"Define *funky*." Ashley peered at her over the edge of her sunglasses.

"I don't know." She wasn't an IT professional. She turned the laptop on, she typed, she uploaded to her blog. That left plenty of uncharted territory. "Plus, the internet connection on this island sucks."

"You're on a minuscule island in the middle of a really big ocean. You're not getting a T1 connection here."

Shutting the lid, Maddie gave up on getting any more work done. She could write tonight in bed. Or tomorrow. She'd managed to feed the internet yet another picture of Mr. Fantasy Fodder, so she'd log back in later to see how her readers had reacted to the butt shot. The bartender walked by, carrying a bucket of limes, and she discreetly leaned around to give him the once-over.

Darn it. None of the few available men on the island stacked up against Mason. The bartender had been her last hope because she'd already checked the others out. One by one. Bottom line? She was desperate and pathetic—and couldn't stop thinking about Mason.

Ashley sighed. "No more work? Or is scoping out the local scenery part of your job description?"

Maddie snorted. "If you make me laugh too hard, I'll wheeze," she warned. Conveniently, she had both her inhaler and a replacement inhaler in her bag by her feet, but why break out the meds if she didn't have to? "We have to be the last two single people here," she complained when Ashley didn't say anything.

The other woman grinned. "You're not my type."

"Thanks." Maddie poked her. "Not even if the world came to an end and we were the last two people standing?"

"If zombies surround the island, I'll reconsider," Ashley promised. "So...you decided to pass on the handsome hottie chef?"

He was a really good kisser. He knew exactly how to touch her and he didn't seem to mind her sass. In fact, he seemed to like it. Like *her*. That possibility sent her up in flames.

"He's playing hard to get," she admitted.

"He's a guy. How hard can he be? Wait." Ashley made a face. "That sounds pornographic. I take it back."

"Too late." Having a vacation girlfriend was fun. Maddie hoped she and Ashley would stay in touch after they both left the island.

"Besides," she continued, "this is a workcation, not a vacation. I should be focusing on my blog, not getting distracted by Mason's butt."

Ashley snorted. "Granted, the man does have a great ass."

"Yeah, but how does it rank in comparison to paying the electric? I need to hit the ball out of the park on my blog, so that's where I should be focusing. Right?"

"When's the last time you had great sex?"

"Full disclosure?" Maddie considered opening the

laptop again. This would make great content. "It's been so long that I'm rusty. Instead of lube, I'm going to need WD-40."

Ashley gestured toward the pool boy. He was a tall, good-looking guy, muscled but still lean. He moved with a lazy confidence that promised great sex with no strings attached, so he certainly ticked all the right boxes. Unfortunately, he was the marzipan in her sexual fantasies, pretty to look at but nothing she actually wanted to eat. Which meant she was, apparently, Team Mason all the way.

Ashley nodded knowingly, then examined the pool guy herself. "So the question is, does anybody else do it for you, or is this a Mason-specific thing?"

She knew the answer to that one.

"Stop looking at that dude's ass." *Busted. Please let him* not *have heard that crack about his butt.* A pair of hands closed over Maddie's eyes, eclipsing her view of the pool boy bending over a stack of towels and effectively blindfolding her. The move was probably unprofessional. Except—she was practically a Fantasy Island employee herself, wasn't she, if she was blogging about them for money? Did that make it better? She'd have to think about that.

"Earth to Maddie. No imagining the staff naked." The amused male voice in her ear recalled her to her current situation. Blindfolded and—*almost*—wrapped in Mason's arms. If that wasn't fantasy fodder, she didn't know what was.

"Are you offering alternatives?"

"My ass is at your disposal," he said drily.

And didn't that make her breathless? Bringing her hands up, she tugged on his wrist. Of course Mason was as immovable as a brick wall, although she was 100 percent certain that said wall lacked Mason's sex appeal. Which she really appreciated. Along with all that warm, male skin. She rubbed her fingers over his smooth inner wrist, bumping against his dive watch.

"I could be convinced to get my kinky on," she murmured.

Totally true, except he was already removing his hands from her eyes. Darn it. Through a fog of lust—which she was *so* not admitting to—she heard Ashley call her goodbyes and disappear. *Chicken.*

"You're incorrigible," he growled. "Come on."

"No more blindfold games?" Because she was all for expanding her horizons and exploring her inner sex kitten. Or just having a really, really good time with Mason. Outlining a few possible bedroom options seemed like fun, but he was already striding away from her.

"You can't tease a girl and then not wait for her." Hopping off her lounger, she grabbed her laptop and her bag and scurried after him as fast as her espadrilles would allow. It wasn't terribly dignified, but Mason in a playful mood was appealing, and they both knew she had no willpower. He smelled like coconut and spice today, which was another vote in his favor. Mason always smelled so good—how could she resist?

When she caught up with him, she slid her hand into his. Mason stared at their linked fingers, no expression visible on his face. Playing poker with him would be inadvisable, unless it was a game of strip poker and she wanted to lose. Making a mental note of that new, fabulous idea, she reached up with her free hand and poked at the corner of his mouth. He raised a brow.

She shrugged. "You should smile when we're holding hands."

"Is that what we're doing?" He looked down at where they were joined and a shiver worked its way up her spine, her nipples doing a little happy-to-see-Mason dance. She'd bet he knew it, too, because when he dragged his gaze back up her body, he paused at her bikini top.

"What else would you call this?" She held their hands up.

"Towing me?" But a smile quirked the corner of his mouth. And, okay, somehow she *was* in front of him, leading. The guy wasn't wrong.

"You don't even know where we're going," he pointed out, taking over.

"What's the point in going slow?"

"Someday, I'm going to show you."

"Promises," she said lightly. That was the problem with Mason. He said these *things*, but then he didn't follow up. So it was entirely possible that he did just see her as one of the guys, and that his teasing was just that—teasing—and not a preview of coming attractions.

He led her inside the resort's gourmet restaurant. It was closed right now in the three-hour window between lunch and dinner, but its emptiness made it easier to appreciate the way it fronted the lagoon with picture-perfect views of the water. It was a romantic place to dine, with rattan furniture, white tablecloths and crystal. Her first thought was that he wanted to show her a new place setting. Or point out the view. Maybe even run a menu by her, which might be fun. But...other than Mason and herself, the restaurant was empty—

except for the cakes lined up with neat precision on a table. Five miniature, ornate, magazine-worthy wedding cakes.

"Is there going to be some mass cultlike wedding later today? Because I have to admit, that wasn't quite how I imagined my wedding."

Dropping her hand, he exhaled roughly, as if maybe she'd pushed him a wee bit too far. When she sneaked a peek at his face, however, he looked as calm and controlled as always. Which was too bad. She really liked the idea of Mason hot and bothered. Out of his element. She fidgeted with her top, smoothing the V that exposed her boobs, and his eyes dipped briefly.

Gotcha.

"You write a wedding blog," he said, as if that explained everything.

"Give the man a cookie."

"So I asked the pastry chef to bake you some cakes. You can sample them for the blog. Take some pictures." He shrugged as though it was no big deal, but it had to have taken hours to bake and decorate these. And he'd convinced the pastry chef to do this for her? Holy. Wow. Impulsively, she threw her arms around him and hugged him. Then equally quickly let go. The man's mad organizational skills were *not* an invitation to touch, although they were technically dating, right? In a normal universe, that meant she got snuggling privileges. While her imagination started fantasizing some creative and potentially naughty scenarios, she set her bag on the floor, grabbed her camera and got busy.

"Describe each one for me." She zoomed in for a close-up.

He pointed. "Lemon. Red velvet. White chocolate with raspberry. Coconut and lime. Vanilla."

Those weren't descriptions. They were lists. Of adjectives. It was kind of cute.

"Do you guys bake a lot of wedding cakes here?"

He shrugged, as though he'd produced a tray of simple cupcakes. "The pastry chef baked these. He didn't complain, so we're good."

He grabbed a knife and a plate and advanced on Cake Row, clearly ready to start slicing and dicing.

She grabbed the hem of his T-shirt. "Wait. It seems a shame to eat them."

"Cake is for eating. I can get more."

God. She could love a man like that. Who knew cake was so bad for her? Without waiting for an answer, he expertly sliced her a thin wedge from each cake and motioned her to a table. She felt a surge of something, and it wasn't just cake lust. She sat on the edge of the table and the first bite was heaven. Lemon and vanilla. Not too heavy and just the right amount of frosting with some kind of almond cream between the layers. Possibly she moaned, because he grinned.

She was halfway through the second slice when she realized he was leaning against the wall, watching her. She liked cake. She wasn't afraid to own that, although she definitely got the feeling that she might like Mason even more. His gaze dropped to her mouth as she slid the frosting-covered tines between her lips.

"You're not eating." Granted, he didn't *look* as though he ate cake. A body like his probably came from a diet of wheatgrass and protein bars.

He looked calm and unruffled, a sexy ocean of cool. She'd dated good-looking guys before. But Mason was different. He was actually a nice guy. Thoughtful. Sweet in a take-it-or-leave-it kind of way. She budged the cake on her plate toward him. Nope. Cake wasn't what she wanted at all.

"I'm not hungry."

"Hello? Cake. Hungry isn't a prerequisite."

He reached down and snagged a bite of hers. "Satisfied?"

Not even a little.

"This is fantastic," she said, giving up on the idea of self-restraint and moving on to the third slice.

A grin tugged at his mouth. "You're the expert."

"I am. Do you have any idea of how many weddings I've been to in the past year?"

"I'm sure you're going to tell me."

"Thirteen."

He smiled. "That's a lot of cake."

"Yeah." She pointed to her butt. "And I'm packing most of it with me."

His gaze dipped south for a moment. "Then, cake is a good look for you."

Perfect answer.

"Let's play twenty questions," she said, needing to distract herself before she said something she regretted.

He gave her an amused look. "Is this where you ask me boxers or briefs? Or how I feel about kinky sex?"

"I won't ask you anything I won't answer myself," she said instead of *yes, please.* She could show some restraint.

"You don't seem to have much of a filter," he said, and she couldn't tell if it was merely an observation or a complaint. He folded his arms over his chest and leaned back. He did that a lot—put himself on the sidelines and just watched. She preferred to be in the center of things.

"Tell me about your sisters." She'd start him off with the easy stuff. She had plenty of practice with getting-to-know-you stuff. The thirteen bridesmaid gigs had meant thirteen groomsmen to chat up.

Mason hesitated, and her internal warning system blared an alert. She realized he didn't have to share personal details with her, but she craved that kind of closeness, too.

"Are the details a state secret? Are they performing superninja stealth missions for Uncle Sam?" She licked the frosting off the fork and eyed the fourth slice that was pink and white with a caramelized raspberry. "Hint…you already told me how many siblings you have, unless you've buried one in the basement and are debating whether or not you should include her in your count. Older? Younger? Let's start there."

"All older." His mouth curved up in a rueful grin. "I'm an uncle a half dozen times over. I'm also your man if you need a makeup test dummy, someone to paint your nails or muscle to explain dating rules to your boyfriend."

"How many are married?" She forked up another bite of cake. God. How could this slice be even better than the other two?

"Three of them. The fourth's still looking." He clenched his jaw. "Personally, I don't think anyone's good enough for any of them, but I was told my opinion didn't count."

"You'd interview every guy in your hometown for her, wouldn't you?"

"That's my job, although San Francisco is a big place."

"You're from the city?"

"Originally," he said. "I've moved around some for work."

"I'm from Burlington," she mumbled around a mouthful of cake that was so good that her eyes might just possibly be rolling back in her head. Whatever culinary school he'd gone to had taught him magic. "In Vermont. And, in case you were planning on asking, we *don't* have more cows than people there. We're a perfectly respectable lakeside city."

"Duly noted." He deftly sliced a third cake, sliding the fluffy wedge onto a clean plate. "Coconut," he said. "With pineapple cream in between the layers."

"Have you lived in San Francisco all your life?"

He shook his head. "We moved there after my father died. He was a hotshot firefighter until he was killed in a wildfire flashover. My mom packed up my sisters and me and took us to a house in Ocean Beach. Nine hundred square feet. One bathroom. Five women and me. I'm surprised the neighbors didn't call us in to the cops once a week just for the noise."

"You? Breaking the law? I'm shocked." She took a bite of cake and moaned.

He ran his thumb over the corner of her mouth, capturing an errant trace of frosting. "There's plenty you don't know about me, sweetheart."

"I'll play. Did you get your start as a chef in San Francisco?"

With a mischievous grin, Maddie pulled her legs up to her chest, hugging her knees to herself because God forbid she use an actual chair. Her bikini was little more than a strip of white wrapped around her boobs with another tease-worthy strip hugging her ass. The sarong thing appeared to be held together by a series of big, loopy bows that had his fingers itching to unwrap her. The thin fabric revealed more than it concealed, starting with a spray of sun freckles that began on her chest, and he wanted to kiss his way up. Distracting her from asking any more questions would be an added bonus.

"Red velvet and yes, in San Francisco," he said and handed her another plate. Surprising her with thoughtful gestures and presents? Another item checked off the perfect-boyfriend list.

She scowled at him as if he was the devil passing out apples in the Garden of Eden. "Your metabolism isn't fair."

If he was smart, he wouldn't touch that one. He knew how much PT he did each day. His body was a tool. A means to get the job done. *Concentrate on slicing the cake. Don't think about kissing her.*

"When's the last wedding you went to?" she asked, licking frosting off her lower lip.

My own. Yeah. That wasn't the answer she was gunning for and he didn't need a *Cosmo* article to know that bringing up his ex wouldn't endear him to Maddie. There was no explaining how naive he'd been at eighteen. Raised to be a stand-up guy, he'd dropped to one knee as soon as he got his high school diploma, produced a ring for his first girlfriend and popped the question. She'd accepted, but neither of them had been really ready for what had come after the vows. He'd done his best, including joining the Navy, because that had seemed like his best shot at a steady paycheck.

That early marriage had ended in annulment two

years after he'd shipped out. He'd been away from home more often than not, and the long separations had been hard on Bethany. He hadn't known how to fix it, so they'd let each other go and moved on. It was water under the bridge, and it had taught him some important lessons about relationships. He still loved sex and appreciated a beautiful woman—he just had one rule. *Don't fall in love.* Besides, getting shot, stabbed and banged up was worth it because keeping people like Maddie safe was the most important thing he could ever do.

Instead of answering, he shoved a piece of cake into her mouth with his fingers. Maddie, being Maddie, couldn't just eat it and maybe tell him it was the best cake ever. Instead, she curled her tongue around his finger and—Jesus—sucked his finger clean. He felt the sensual tug all the way to his dick, and possibly somewhere a little more north. Like his heart.

Since that was dangerously close to violating the don't-fall-in-love rule, he did something out of character. He traced her cleavage with a frosting-covered finger. She didn't pull back, either, as he drew a swirl of sugar and cream over her skin. Just watched the progress of his finger as he skimmed lower.

"Are we friends?"

He thought about that for a moment, then thought about pressing his mouth against the sweet spot he'd created. Licking her clean—or very, very dirty—definitely trumped anything else he'd rather be doing right now.

"Absolutely," he said, confused.

"*Just* friends?" She narrowed her eyes and he got the feeling that his answer mattered a hell of a lot. *Back it up, sailor.* If the answer mattered, he wanted to give it some thought.

"Why are you asking?"

"I feel the need to check because—" she shrugged, as if it was no big deal, as if he wasn't stroking his finger up and down the warm V of her breasts "—I've made this mistake before."

"We're a mistake?"

Because he really didn't think so.

She blushed, the bright pink a really interesting combination with her red hair. It was actually kind of cute, although he'd bet she was mad about the blush. Maddie liked being in control, and she definitely preferred being the person saying something outrageous. He kind of liked being the one to shock her for a change.

Funny how smiling seemed to be his usual condition when he was around Maddie. She made him feel good. She also made him hard but, if he was really lucky, she might be willing to help him with that particular problem.

"I'd like to have sex with you," he admitted gruffly, withdrawing his finger and stepping closer. "I'd also like to get to know you better, because I like you. The friends part is good, too."

"Friends with possibilities," she said, sounding happy.

He felt a surge of something he decided to label as lust, and reached for her sarong. The little bow-tie knot had been driving him crazy. Thank God she tied lousy knots. One firm tug and the fabric parted, pooling around her so she just sat there cross-legged in her bikini.

"You want to have possibilities right *here*?" She sounded slightly scandalized. Good. Usually he was the one off balance around Maddie. It was nice to return the favor.

He flashed a grin. "Are you offering?"

"Maybe." Her eyes darted around the restaurant. "But it seems kind of unhygienic to have sex on a table where people eat."

He couldn't help it. He laughed. "You really don't have a filter, do you?"

"Hey, I call it like I see it." She leaned back on her elbows, propping one foot up on his shoulder. She had a tattoo inked over her left hip. He'd noticed it before, but he'd never been close enough to read the words hidden in the delicate swirl of flowers and…feathers. She had freakin' feathers tattooed on her hip. Feathers that were excessive and bold and one flourish after another. He liked it.

He liked *her*, and damn if that wasn't a dangerous thought.

"You have a tattoo." He brushed his thumb gently over her ink. She felt just as silky and warm there as she did elsewhere. The only difference was on the surface of things.

"Uh-huh." She twisted to look down at the pink-and-black words scrolling over her hip. "'More than a catbird hates a cat.'"

"Two questions." Hooking a chair with his foot, he drew it closer and dropped down on it. This gave him the best-ever view of her inner thighs. Plus, her bikini bottom barely covered her generous curves, and just knowing that only a few inches of nylon separated him from her pussy drove him crazy. He was pretty sure she knew it, too.

"Really? You want to ask questions *now*?" She definitely sounded breathless.

Apparently he did. He slid his hands underneath her ass and her whole body quivered in response. "Why?"

"Why get a tattoo?" She leaned up farther on her elbows. "Because…I…uh…could. Because sometimes people *do* things in college because there may have been too many beers and too much encouragement. Because…I have a thing for Ogden Nash."

He untied the left string of her bikini. "Are any of those reasons true?"

She flushed. "All of them. Have I ever lied to you?"

No. That was him.

"Never," he said, shifting closer and running a thumb over the silky soft skin of her inner thigh.

Her husky moan was followed by yet another question. They needed to work on the whole keeping-quiet thing. "How about you? Any ink on you?"

"Never." He must have stiffened because she made a sympathetic face and patted him on the arm. As if he was five. *Jesus.*

"Not a needle man?"

He'd seen horrific injuries and kept right on doing his job. But show him a 28-gauge needle and he got light-headed. He puked. After getting his jabs as an enlisted man, he'd actually passed out on the nurse. So yeah, he got more than a little green just thinking about her tattoo.

Deflect. "Did it hurt?"

"If I say yes, are you going to kiss it better?" She sounded breathless again.

"No," he said. "I'm going to kiss you."

"Works for me," she purred.

That made two of them. He undid the right string, and, God, he loved her swimsuits. The silky panel fell away and he'd never seen a prettier sight than her landing strip of dark red hair. He didn't have any words for the scent of her, but she was amazing. She didn't seem to mind that he had his face inches from her pussy. He liked that confidence. She planned to enjoy him, and apparently had no problem with letting him in on her anticipation.

"Like what you see? FYI, I'm a natural redhead." Her voice sounded even huskier than usual, which he decided to interpret as approval of their game.

"You're gorgeous." If he couldn't be honest about who he was or why he was on Fantasy Island, he didn't want there to be any doubt about *this*. She was damned beautiful and he wanted to make this memorable for her. If she wanted to play erotic games, he'd do his best. *Hooyah.*

He reached over and slicked his finger with frosting.

"Are we getting creative?" She settled back on the table. He decided to interpret that as "carry on."

"I thought you liked my cake."

Not waiting for her answer, he spread her open. She was pink and glistening, clinging to his finger when he gave in to temptation and had to touch. Because looking definitely wasn't enough. Hell, this *afternoon* wasn't going to be enough. Not for him.

"Mason." His name came out part moan, part breathy sigh.

"Mason, stop—or Mason, do it some more?" While he waited for her answer, he drew his frosting-covered finger down over her stomach, painted the sweetest of arrows to her own sweet spot. When he followed his path with his mouth, licking the frosting from her skin until he'd moved entirely between her thighs, she moaned again.

"Definitely 'Mason, do it some more,'" she whispered pleadingly.

Grunting his approval, he swirled his tongue in small circles around the sensitive spot. She cried out, pushing up into his touch, so he did it again. Spread her wider, drank her in. She was so goddamned pretty and open, and right now she was also all his.

"You know what I have to do now." He met her gaze, knowing his voice was low and rough, but, damn, she drove him crazy. He had no idea how he'd walk away without tasting her now.

"Do it *faster*," she demanded.

He leaned forward with a laugh, pushing her thighs wider with his hands, close enough to smell the vanilla of the frosting and that musky, perfect scent that was all Maddie. "Maddie."

He ran his tongue down her slick folds. He had a feeling that, from now on, he'd get a hard-on whenever he smelled vanilla. She was gorgeous opening up for him.

"Mason." Good. He liked his name on her tongue, but he wanted more. More response, more Maddie, more *orgasm*. He inserted a finger inside her. Her soft, hot channel clung to his finger. "Mason, stop or Mason, more?"

She pushed against his finger. "You're so slow."

"And you like it." He moved his finger deeper.

"More. Now." She wriggled demandingly.

The table couldn't possibly be comfortable, so he scooped her up and deposited her on the padded banquette seat. It wasn't as good as having her in his bed, but it was an improvement. She wouldn't thank him if she had bruises on her gorgeous ass tomorrow, and he already knew he wanted to see her again like this.

"Shh. Let me give you what you want."

GOD. THE MAN could kiss. The frosting thing was more sticky and funny than sexy. She wasn't sure she was cut out for kink, because she'd had to fight back giggles when he'd grabbed a fingerful of frosting, but then she was really glad she'd been willing to humor him because, holy moly, he'd painted her body as if she was the Sistine Chapel and he was Michelangelo. The erotic pressure had sent sensation shooting through her body. The skin of his thumb was rough and callused, as if he used his hands for plenty more than cooking. He touched her with short strokes, sensual appetizers that made her want more and, if he was decorating her like a cake, then surely he planned on licking her clean? *Please.*

She leaned back. Part of her wanted to watch him, to see that dark head bent over her pussy, but the rest of her just melted. She wanted this, wanted *him,* and apparently he felt the same way. Just the thought aroused her more.

His tongue stroked down. Up. She stopped worrying that he had her spread out in circumstances a little too public for her own tastes. But his tongue… God, the man's tongue was magic. He licked her, ravished her as though she was his own very special, tasty treat and she dug her heels into his shoulders and let him.

Not sure where to put her hands, she jammed her fingers into her mouth because screaming wouldn't be wise. Acquiring an audience now would suck. He stripped away her reasons to care, to hold back, be-

cause there was room only for the two of them and all
that incredible, exquisite pleasure. The pleasure built
and built, and all her attention focused on that one
sweet, aching spot he circled with his tongue. Sucked
with his wicked, talented mouth. Her whole world narrowed to the man making her come apart.

The sounds of voices talking and laughing had no
place in her fantasy and jerked her back to awareness
of her surroundings. Mason lifted his head, his fingers
cupping her possessively. "Someone's coming," she
whispered, as if keeping her voice down could hide
what they were doing here.

She could kill them. Her body was a tight, wet, puls-
ing ache and she was so damned close. The need to
come was a fierce demand, but they weren't alone.

"Then, you'd better be quick," he growled. "Because
you didn't say *stop*."

She swiped her telltale swimsuit bottom from the
top of the table. They were going to get busted. She'd
die of embarrassment. But the arousal was there, too,
and a growing sense of excitement. She wouldn't have
guessed Mason had this devilish side to him. "You
can't be serious."

He gave her that small half smile. "We're not done
here."

Then he curled his fingers, finding a spot inside her
that made her body feel like Fourth of July fireworks.
She felt her resistance—what there'd been of it—melt
away. In the distance, someone called to him.

"I'll be there in a minute," he yelled. Then, to her,
he said, "Faster."

"What about you?"

She didn't take orders. Honestly, she was more the

type to give them. Except… Just looking at him made her wet. He was a big, broad-shouldered shadow looming over her, standing between her and discovery. Maybe this could work.

"You don't worry about me." He stroked his fingers deeper, finding a spot that had her breath whimpering out of her and her heels drilling into his back. *So good.* "This is for you."

Okay. She could work with that.

His head descended again and she held her breath. Listening. Anticipating. He pressed against her again and the sensation was just as good as before. His mouth tickled and set her on fire, sensation shooting through her. It was almost more personal now that it wasn't just the two of them, not just their game. Someone could come in, could catch them, and then…then she had no idea. *Faster,* he'd ordered.

She arched her back, digging her heels in as she pushed up, hips rising to meet his mouth. His tongue moved faster, harder, stroking and circling her clit in a maddening pattern. She jammed a hand into her mouth because if she screamed, if other people knew…she had no idea, but then all thought flew out of her head as the tremors built and built, her body flying apart because suddenly she was right *there.* Coming for him as he pressed the heel of his hand hard against her, riding the wave of pleasure with him.

"Gorgeous," he whispered hoarsely, lifting himself away from her. "If only I had more time, sweetheart."

Yes. If only. If only they had more time. If only she could hold on to this moment forever. She tugged free, determined not to lose a second. Grinning because, damn, he made her feel good, she brushed a kiss over his mouth and pulled her swimsuit bottom back on. He had to get going, but the heat in his eyes warmed her. She wasn't quite ready to let him go. Not yet.

She pulled back, easing up on her grip on his T-shirt. "Maybe we'll see each other soon?"

He cupped her face, gave her another quick, hot kiss. The sensation of his fingertips brushing her skin was electric. He'd touched her, made her come with those same fingers, but her body tightened and quickened, already eager for more of this man.

"I'd like that," he said huskily. "I'd really like that."

Me, too, she thought, sliding off the table and forcing herself to walk away. *I'd like that, too.*

7

Okay, ladies. Advice time! Mr. Fantasy Fodder isn't one for chitchat (think Tall, Dark, and Almost Always Silent), but when he *does* smile and say something, I can't help but notice. He actually has a wicked sense of humor and gets this little twinkle in his eye when something amuses him. Yay for melting girl parts! Our chemistry is off the charts. Is this what you all felt when you met The One? Was your bedroom rocking from the get-go? Because FF seemed a little reluctant to get entirely naked with yours truly. Not that I wouldn't have let him keep *some* clothes on (adventuresome is good!), but the possibility that he wasn't sure if he really wanted to go to bed with me is a downer. Especially since the man really, really knows what to do with frosting. My lips are sealed, but the memories... I'll just say that FF definitely lived up to his nickname and I'd like to get to know him biblically. Send advice stat!

—MADDIE, Kiss and Tulle

MASON POUNDED ALONG the jungle trail, working through mile five of his morning PT. The sound of his boots hitting ground was a familiar rhythm, but everything else about the morning was off. He'd organized *cakes*, for crying out loud. Really girlie, over-the-top, flower-and-frosting numbers with little plastic bride and groom dolls perched on top. He'd be making cupcakes and whipping out the Easy-Bake Oven next.

Levi had laughed his ass off. Of course, the man had also been quick to steal leftovers, too, so Mason's cakes clearly hadn't been the worst idea ever. Somehow, somewhere, he'd metamorphosed into Military Martha Stewart, worried about how his batter had come out and if Maddie would approve.

Bottom line? He had it bad.

Granted, getting close to her was a mission requirement, but *she* didn't know that. All this getting-to-know-you crap had been genuine on her part. She'd decided that he might qualify as dating material and now she was performing her due diligence on his personality and bona fides with the same enthusiasm she approached everything else.

It didn't take a rocket scientist to figure out that Maddie didn't hide what she was feeling. She just *enjoyed* and went for it. The girl didn't hold back sexually, either, which meant it didn't take too much imagination at all for him to mentally transfer Maddie's enthusiasm to the bedroom. She'd rock his world if he was lucky enough to get the chance. Putting her back together after he'd gotten her off yesterday had been one of the hardest things he'd ever done. He'd wanted to scoop her up, carry her off to somewhere with a bed and crawl in with her for hours. Days. As long as she'd have him.

God help him if she ever figured out why he was really on Fantasy Island, because she'd kill him. He knew without asking that Maddie had a zero-tolerance policy on lying, and sins of omission would count every bit as much as the real whoppers. So he'd make sure she didn't find out. He was a trained professional. He'd successfully conducted hundreds of covert missions.

And…no amount of training or hands-on experience in the field could fix the basic problem. He wasn't *acting* when he was around Maddie. She knew that he was interested and, hooyah, his interest was genuine. His perpetual erection when he was around her had to be one of his worst-kept secrets ever. The kissing and the touching didn't help in the keeping-things-under-control department, either. But he felt as if he was negotiating under false pretenses. In another time, another place, he'd have happily gone after her, but here on Fantasy Island, sticking closer than close to her was essential for her safety. The recon team still hadn't confirmed Santiago's presence in the jungle compound, which meant the bastard could potentially be anywhere. Money also bought loyalty and guns. A Marcos bodyguard or a hired mercenary could easily slip onto the island, so that meant Mason stayed nearby.

Practically glued skin to skin with the sexy, gorgeous, uninhibited Maddie.

He picked up speed, but outrunning Maddie's charms wasn't a matter of pacing. It was already hot and humid, his T-shirt sticking to him as he began the upward climb. He'd turn around at the lookout, head back to the resort and relieve Levi. Levi had Maddie watch until Mason tagged back in, so she was in good hands.

Exhaustion tugged at him. He'd survived on less

sleep, but banking some hours was wise. Pulling an all-nighter would be easier if he wasn't already sleep deprived. *Suck it up, sailor.* He checked the dive watch strapped to his wrist, already knowing that his pace was too slow. He pushed harder, his head clearing as his blood got pumping. Failure simply wasn't an option.

When he reached the top of the hill, he did a quick check, but Maddie either hadn't sneaked any more cameras up here or she'd gotten a whole lot more strategic at placing them. It was just him, some palm trees and an enormous round lounger thing with cushions and a little canopy for shade. He stopped and stretched, working out the tension in his back. Blue lagoon spread out before him, stretching to the reef and beyond. Maddie had rocked a blue, fringed bikini the other day that was just that kind of peacock color.

And, wait for it… His erection tented his pants, right on cue.

He'd walked by the pool yesterday. Taken in the cabana scene. Looked again because, damn, the itty-bitty bikini had almost *not* covered Maddie's stunning curves and he'd wanted to run his fingers over all that lush, tempting skin. Then she'd bent over, rummaging in an enormous beach bag for something, and his brain had completely short-circuited. The Brazilian swimsuit bottom absolutely, positively failed to cover her ass. He'd fought the urge to cup those naughty curves in his palms. The bottom of her suit had a wicked seam that ran up her butt, kind of like an X-marks-the-spot.

He'd stood there like a different kind of ass. For several very long, heated moments. Then she'd busted him with a wicked grin.

"Tell me if you spot a tan line."

Yeah. He'd about swallowed his tongue. True that there were no white marks anywhere *he* could see, but the mental image had made him want to strip off the nylon scraps and explore for himself. Do a double-check. Maybe rub some sunscreen on, because it would be a crime to burn her pretty skin.

"Nothing to say?" She'd flopped onto a lounger, lying down on her belly and then—his all-time favorite memory of the day—had reached up to tug the strings undone. The skimpy fabric had fallen away, exposing the generous curve of her breasts.

He'd growled out a "Carry on" and beaten a hasty retreat, the big, bad SEAL run off by a string bikini.

Another wave of exhaustion battered at him. He hadn't slept more than a couple of hours these past few days and he'd be no good to her if he passed out standing up. The empty lounger seemed like his best bet. Palming his secure phone, he texted Levi.

Is HRH covered?

The odds of Maddie being awake at shortly after sunrise seemed minimal.

Sure enough, Levi responded almost immediately.

Sleeping. I can be inside in two if she needs a good-night kiss.

His reaction was instinctive—and telling.

Hands off.

And of course Levi ran with it.

No hands. Got it. Tongue okay?

Never leave that SEAL a loophole. Instead, he went for honesty.

I'm out for an hour.

After Levi confirmed that he'd keep watch over Maddie and no one—not even the zombie overlord in the yet-to-happen zombie apocalypse—would get to her, Mason let himself relax. He dropped onto the lounger and rolled over, concealing the handgun tucked against the small of his back. This early in the morning, none of the resort guests should be up and about—they seemed to prefer Maddie's version of early morning, which kicked off at lunchtime—but better safe than sorry. Monkeys and birds chatted back and forth in the treetops, and the faint pounding of the surf traveled across the lagoon. Yeah. He'd slept in worse places. This would do.

He set his internal clock and let sleep take him.

FANTASY ISLAND CAME with a sleeping beauty.

If Maddie had known Mason was the reward for early-morning exercise, she'd have jumped out of bed. He looked downright edible—and sound asleep. Poor baby. She stepped off the path and into the lookout point. Just as pretty as it had been the other morning, when Mason had startled her and she'd lost her memory card. Calm blue lagoon with a clear view of the fringing reef. Lots of palm trees and just a slice of white sugary beach. She was looking at calendar material.

The man didn't hurt, either. She told herself that

her heart banging in her ears had nothing to do with Sleeping Beauty, even if he did look cute, sprawled facedown on the love seat. When he didn't so much as twitch as she approached, she checked to make sure he was breathing—which he was, because his lungs were undoubtedly as fit as the rest of him—and then checked out his mighty fine ass in his cargo pants. He wore the usual pair of industrial-strength boots and the fitted cotton T-shirt that seemed to be his wardrobe staple when he wasn't sporting chef whites. Today he looked like a mixed-martial-arts champion or someone else suitably large and rough around the edges. The only thing missing was a sleeve of tattoos. God, she loved a good tattoo.

Almost perfect, but not quite…

Huh. Maybe that could be fixed.

She rummaged in her bag—the joys of being prepared—and fished out a stick of sunscreen. She was an excellent almost girlfriend, because this was classy colored sunscreen that came with cartoon characters on the tube. But really, she had a problem. What to write? The thick, corded arm over his face severely restricted the amount of available real estate. His other arm stretched across his head. She looked up at the sky. Perfect. It was like having her very own darkroom—he'd be sporting her extraspecial message in about another hour. Delicately, she finger painted a word onto his arm, outlining three perfect letters in the cream. *H-O-T.*

She was just settling in to enjoy herself when Mason came awake. One minute, her sleeping beauty was sprawled out in a power nap, and the next he'd rolled, pulling her beneath him and pinning her wrists with one hand. His hand gripped her jaw, the other pressed over her throat.

Oh. My. God. Mental note: don't poke the sleeping giant.

The sunscreen fell from her hand as her heart kicked into overdrive. Mason looked…scary. And she wasn't entirely sure she could breathe.

"It's just me," she said hoarsely.

He blinked and looked down at her. He didn't ease up on his grip on her jaw. "Maddie?"

She twisted her head, trying to dislodge his hand. *Downplay it.* "Somebody wakes up grumpy."

He stared down at her, as if he had no idea how he'd ended up on top of her. She'd draw him a diagram—later. She wriggled, because the position had both possibilities and some serious drawbacks. Breathing, for instance, fell into the drawback category. Her man seriously outweighed her and it felt as though a water buffalo had parked himself on her boobs. Taking a deep breath was impossible.

Help.

"Maddie?" The way he rasped her name in a sleep-roughened voice fell into the possibilities column. He whipped his hand away from her throat, a move she appreciated even as she made a mental note to never, ever poke him awake in the middle of the night. "Fuck."

"I'm good with that," she said, because making a joke was so much better than dealing with unwelcome trembling she couldn't quite stop. When had Mason gotten so fierce looking? "If you're volunteering to put out."

He didn't look particularly pleased to see her, but he also didn't wear his emotions on his face. She wiggled again, to remind him that she was still pinned beneath him—with the water buffalo parked on her chest. And, thank you, downtown interest from Mason. She also had to wonder why he still hadn't let go of her wrists.

"Are we playing domination games? Because I've never done that before. You could be my first."

He sprang off her, and *that* was about as far from flattering as it was possible to get.

"Did I hurt you? Can you breathe?"

She took a quick inventory because he looked so serious. It was cute, the way he worried. "I'm a little more 2-D than 3-D at the moment, but I'll live. And I've got my inhaler if I need it."

He thunked his head back on the lounger and groaned. He hadn't been all that rough, so she had no idea what his problem was. Maybe he was still wrestling with his inner gentleman—in which case, she was probably the one who needed to do the apologizing, because her inner bad girl had come out days ago with one goal and one goal only: get Mason into bed.

He pushed up on one elbow. She, on the other hand, was content to lie there and stare up at him. Who needed to get all energetic about things? Not only was he gorgeous when he was all sleepy and rumpled, but his eyes held a concern that she liked all too much. She really didn't think she was just a convenient vacation hookup for him. Really. She didn't.

Or maybe that was just more wishful thinking on her part.

"No bruises. No broken bones," she said cheerfully. "In fact, I'm as good as new."

He rubbed his thumb over her throat, smoothing the skin he'd strong-armed. "Hurting you is the last thing I want to do. You need to be careful when I'm asleep. I don't—"

"Wake up well?" Understatement. On the other hand, his words sure implied he planned on doing some more waking up around her, and just the thought had her heart hammering at her rib cage, as if the thing could leap straight out and into Mason's arms. If she was lucky, the waking up would happen after a night of really hot sex. She could suggest a practice session. Or two. Or six…

"Yeah." He dragged a hand down his face. "Look—"

She needed to point one thing out. "If you apologize, I'm going to kill you."

He nodded. "Duly noted, although I feel the need to point out that apologizing would be the polite thing to do."

"Because you pinned me?" She shrugged. "You startled me. I got over it. To be honest, I found it kind of sexy."

He made a choked sound.

See? The man really didn't have serial killer tendencies after all. She'd caught him at a bad moment. That was all.

"I've shocked you." She crossed her arms over her chest. Partly because she needed to do something with her hands, and putting them on Mason's body was apparently not an option this afternoon, but also because the move gave her some serious cleavage. From the way Mason's eyes darkened, he'd definitely noticed. He didn't make a move, though. The man sure had discipline.

She sighed. "You're going to insist on being a gentleman, aren't you?"

"Probably." He stood up. "Come on."

"Where are we going?" *Say to bed*, her inner bad girl begged shamelessly. Because that was where we really want to be.

"I'll walk you back to your place *because* I'm a gentleman," he said, flashing a grin. She made a face. "How can you look like such a bad boy but be such a nice guy?"

MASON AND LEVI had done BUD/S training together before they'd shipped out to the same unit. That practically made them an old married couple, but right now Mason had divorce on his mind. He tracked Levi down and found the guy doing push-ups on the beach. Levi turned his head as Mason stormed the beach.

"What's up?"

He tackled Levi and the man collapsed with a satisfying thud on the sand.

"You couldn't give me a heads-up that Maddie was moving?"

Levi grunted and bucked upward. Mason turned his own head just in time to avoid a fistful of sand aimed at his eyes. Levi fought dirty, which was okay, because Mason was no gentleman, either. No matter what Maddie believed. He rolled, using his weight to pin Levi down.

"We're having a conversation about this," he ground out. He was in a pissy mood and he knew it, but he didn't need Maddie sneaking up on him when he was sleeping. "She was perfectly safe," Levi said, hooking a leg around his. Mason went briefly airborne before his back met the sand. Jesus. That hurt. Wasn't sand

supposed to be soft? Surging up, he went for Levi, pulling the other man back down.

"How do you know that?"

"Because I followed her up that hill. I even waited
while she checked you out, did her thing and you woke
up. Some dating advice? Choking the girl is a guaranteed way to lose the girl unless she's into some really
kinky stuff you'd be better off avoiding."

Okay. So Maddie hadn't been out alone. He let Levi's
head go, enjoying the satisfying thunk when Levi's
skull connected with the sand.

"Also?" Levi continued. "You do realize that woman
is trouble, right? Because the questions you haven't
asked yet are why did she climb that hill and what did
she do before she woke you up."

Huh. From the devilish grin on Levi's face, Maddie
hadn't been engaging in a little healthy exercise. And
he hadn't thought to ask her that. Come to think of it,
she wasn't much for exercise, period.

"Tell me," he demanded.

"Nice memo." Levi pointed to Mason's forearm. "By
midnight, you're going to get the full effect. *H-O-T*
stood out on the suntanned skin of his forearm in fading neon pink letters. He raised his forearm and sniffed
at it. Sunscreen.

"Protection's important," Levi said with mock seri-
ousness. "Next time, take a bath in SPF 1,200 and you
won't have this problem."

Hell. He'd been so off his game, waking up and
finding Maddie pinned beneath him where—no matter what she'd said—he could have hurt her badly. He'd
been trained in all kinds of martial arts and hand-to-
hand-combat techniques, so he'd reacted on instinct

and now he didn't trust himself around her. Not until he could guarantee he *wouldn't* hurt her. Even if hurting her was something he'd never do when he was awake, how did he shut down his gut reactions?

Levi slid him a glance. "You like her."

"What's not to like?" He rolled over onto his back, shading his eyes with his arm. Maybe he was getting too old for this shit. His back hurt. His neck hurt.

"I mean *like* like her." Levi went back to doing push-ups. The man was unstoppable when it came to PT.

"Are we in middle school?"

"If you want to date her for real, date her."

"Are you offering dating advice now?" he scoffed. Levi gave a shoulder shrug and put his right hand on his back before dropping into another set of perfect push-ups. "I've dated recently, which is more than I can say for you."

He started counting off reps.

Following suit, Mason rolled over and straightened his arms, pushing into his first rep. There was no point in wasting valuable PT time.

The thing was, he'd kissed Maddie and enjoyed the hell out of himself. She was someone special, and he wanted the chance at more kisses. And possibly something else, although the *else* part kind of scared him, almost as much as it made him want to wrap his arms around her and hold on. "We kissed," he admitted gruffly. Levi had never struck him as the kind of guy who did *relationships*, but he was desperate. At this point he'd take any advice that didn't come from a stupid magazine column.

Levi counted off another ten push-ups, then hit the

sand for a breather. Thirty seconds recovery, Mason knew, and he'd do another set. "Where?" he asked.

"Are we *girlfriends*? Do you really need details?"

Levi gave him a droll look. "I need to know what I'm working with here. Was this a quick-brush-on-the-cheek kind of kiss, or the kind that involves removing clothing?"

Punching his teammate seemed like the more appealing option at the moment. Instead, he finished his own set of reps, welcoming the burn in his arm muscles. "B," he gritted out.

Levi whistled. "Good for you."

"She thinks I'm boyfriend material."

Levi grinned at him. "And that's a problem? I thought you wanted to get to know her."

"*She* thinks I'm a chef."

Levi shrugged and pushed up. "So? You can cook. It's not false advertising."

Which was splitting hairs. "But I'm not here on Fantasy Island to cook."

"So she gets a side of bonus SEAL. I'm still not seeing the problem."

"I took her laptop," he said through clenched teeth. "There are things I'm not telling her. How do you think she'd feel about that? How would anyone feel?"

Levi sighed. "This would be so much easier if you didn't have a moral compass."

Right. "Not helpful."

"Do you like her?"

Mason examined his arm and the pale words painted onto his skin. He could feel the grin tugging at his mouth. "Yeah. I do."

"So get to know *her*. See where this goes. Maybe it's just a hookup."

"You think she's using me for sex?"

"Would you be complaining? It's *Fantasy* Island. Not Uptight Island, Vestal Virgin Island or Not Tonight Dear Island."

"That was—"

"Crass?" Levi switched arms. "Absolutely. But it's also true. See what she wants. Maybe she just wants to explore her options with you, have a good time. In which case, great. The two of you can go *enjoy* each other and then, when our time's up, you can leave with a clear conscience. But if there's more to it than that and you decide you want to keep seeing her, you'll figure out the logistics later."

"That plan sucks."

"True," Levi acknowledged. "But we both know you're going with it anyhow. Stick with the script and you'll be fine."

"You really think a lousy quiz is going to turn me into the perfect boyfriend?"

Not that he wasn't willing to give it a shot for Maddie, but he was also a realist. He was career military and a SEAL. He was more than a little rough around the edges, and he definitely wasn't domesticated, even if he could cook.

Levi just grinned. "At least you'll get sex out of it, right?"

To hell with PT and push-ups. He launched himself at Levi again. The funny thing was that, in trying to follow the magazine script about being the perfect boyfriend, he was happier than he'd ever been. He liked Maddie. She was funny and brave and bold as hell—

and that was *before* he'd managed to get her into bed. He had no doubts whatsoever that she'd rock his world there, too. But all that sass came with a side of vulnerability. She hid it well, but it was there, and he didn't plan on being the asshole who hurt her more. Levi, on the other hand, was fair game.

"You kiss your mother with that mouth?"

Levi twisted, reversing the hold. "You're fixated on kissing. Do it more. Talk about it less."

"Be respectful," he growled, and followed up the order with a second takedown. Levi hit the sand hard.

Maddie was trying to do a job, and he respected that. After all, he was here on a workcation as well, courtesy of Uncle Sam. A lot of other SEALs would have tried to score with her. She was a stunning woman, downright beautiful, her lush curves a whole lot of sexy. Holding back was the *last* thing he wanted to do.

"Got it." Levi elbowed him. "But I still recommend more kissing."

Yeah. He wanted more kissing, too, but he was also old enough to know that sometimes making out *wasn't* the answer.

Like Maddie, his ex-wife had been fun and the life of the party. He didn't really know what he was supposed to have done differently. They'd gotten married; he'd shipped out. Maybe his mistake had been believing the paycheck and long-distance love would be enough. Maybe expecting her to wait was unrealistic. But he'd said the words in front of her family preacher and he'd meant them. There was nothing wrong with laughter and a good time. He was all for that. He just didn't have any practice at what came after the "I dos" and was batting zero for one in the department of happily-ever-after. Married at eighteen. Divorced at twenty. His kissing experience didn't count for shit.

8

Mr. Fantasy Fodder continues to live up to his name. I'm a very happy camper, although he still seems reluctant to get naked with me. Is there some kind of secret vacation hookup etiquette that I need to learn? Or does he just think I'm not That Kind of Girl? Because, for him, I totally could be, ladies. Fantasy Island has a secret that I'm about to out for you all. The cocktail menu? Isn't just about getting your drunk on. All those sexy, sexy names are bedroom suggestions. If I tell FF to order me a *Long Slow Screw Against the Wall*, he's supposed to take the hint and take *me* up against the wall.

—MADDIE, Kiss and Tulle

AFTER A DAY spent working on her blog, Maddie felt pleasantly virtuous when Mason texted her. Not that the brief You busy? was fantasy fodder. Nope. The fantasy was what had happened the day before yesterday, and although waking him up at the lookout point yes-

The legs were about a mile long. The kind of legs that went beyond wrapping around a guy's waist.

He almost groaned when his eyes reached a pair of black leather boots similar to the ones he wore on duty. Was there anything sexier than legs like that in black boots?

"Hellooo," he murmured.

"What?" The hips moved, the back arched and the owner of those sexy legs lifted her head so fast he heard it hit something under the sink. Rubbing her head, the woman glared at him with enough heat to start a fire.

"Taylor?"

"Cat?" he said at the same time. He started to help her to her feet, but at the last second paused. Touching her so soon after that image of her legs wrapped around him didn't seem like a smart idea.

When the hell had Kitty Cat gotten hot?

Her golden hair was tied back, highlighting a face too strong to be called pretty. Eyes the color of the ocean at sunset stared back under sharply arched brows. The rounded cheeks and slight upper bite were familiar.

The way her faded green tee cupped her breasts was new, as was the sweetly gentle slide from breast to waist to hip where the tee met denim.

Oh, yeah. Kitty Cat was definitely hot.

"Hey there, Mr. Wizard," Cat greeted. "Still out saving the world?"

"As always. How about the Kitty Cat?"

"Same as ever," Cat said with a shrug that did interesting things to that T-shirt of hers.

Things he had no business noticing…

Don't miss A SEAL'S TOUCH by Tawny Weber, available February 2016!

*Navy SEAL Taylor "The Wizard" Powell has a
reputation for getting out of tricky situations. Bad guys,
bombs—no problem. Finding a girlfriend in order to
evade matchmaking friends? Not so easy.*

Taylor Powell pulled his Harley into the driveway and cut the engine.

Home.

He headed for the front door, located his key and stepped inside.

"Yo," he called out as the door swung shut behind him. "Ma?"

He heard a thump then a muffled bang.

"Ma?" His long legs ate up the stairs as he did a quick mental review of his last CPR certification.

As he barreled past his childhood bedroom, he heard another thump coming from the hall bathroom. This time accompanied by cussing.

Very female, very unmotherly, cussing.

In a blink his tension dissipated.

He knew that cussing.

Grinning he sauntered down the hall. Stopping in the bathroom door, he smiled in appreciation of the sweetly curved rear end encased in worn denim.

Love the Harlequin book you just read?

Your opinion matters.

Review this book on your favorite book site, review site, blog or your own social media properties and share your opinion with other readers!

Turn your love of reading into rewards you'll love with

Harlequin My Rewards

THE WORLD IS BETTER WITH

Romance

Harlequin has everything from contemporary, passionate and heartwarming to suspenseful and inspirational stories.

Whatever your mood, we have a romance just for you!

Connect with us to find your next great read, special offers and more.

f /HarlequinBooks

🐦 @HarlequinBooks

www.HarlequinBlog.com

www.Harlequin.com/Newsletters

HARLEQUIN®

A *Romance* FOR EVERY MOOD™

www.Harlequin.com

JUST CAN'T GET ENOUGH?

Join our social communities
and talk to us online.

You will have access to the latest
news on upcoming titles and special
promotions, but most importantly,
you can talk to other fans about your
favorite Harlequin reads.

Harlequin.com/Community

Facebook.com/HarlequinBooks

Twitter.com/HarlequinBooks

Pinterest.com/HarlequinBooks

terday had definitely started off on the wrong foot, the end results hadn't been bad, either.

Since she'd just wrapped things up, she'd texted back, Is that an offer?

Her phone vibrated seconds later.

Thought I'd give you a chance to apologize.

Uh-huh. Fingers flying, she mounted her defense.

For what? I've been a good girl.

He responded with a photo of his forearm. Whoops. She'd forgotten about her arts-and-crafts hoax. He might have a point about the need to atone.

Not that she'd tell him that—or that she'd been dying to see him again. After she'd accidentally on purpose woken him up at the lookout point, he'd walked her back to her bungalow, but he hadn't come in. Hadn't so much as given her a kiss goodbye. Which, okay, had kind of sucked. She'd known he had to work—after all, she did, too—but she'd been disappointed about the brush-off and had been secretly hoping he could carve out some time for them. However, she'd exercised amazing self-control and had resisted chasing him down. His text had been her reward.

When he knocked on her front door, Maddie opened it. Her heart fluttered as she slowly drank him in. The man had the best taste in shirts. Today he wore a faded navy blue T-shirt that hugged his taut chest and exposed his muscular forearms, along with blue jeans that were white around the seams and a pair of rugged black boots. God. She loved boots on a man. She

doubted he'd picked out his clothes with her fantasies in mind, but just the sight of him, rumpled and strong and a little battered around the edges? Yeah. That sight got her going.

"Listen, uh, about the tattoo. If you want it removed—"

Not that she actually had any idea how to fix the letters she'd finger painted onto his arm, but the offer had to count for something, right?

Mason cut her off. "Don't worry about it. We have better things to do." He held up a wicker basket as though it was Exhibit A.

"Picnic?" She eyed the sky doubtfully. "It's dark. Don't picnics require daylight?"

He shrugged. "Since when do you follow all the rules?"

She knew she had a reputation for winging it, but she wasn't sure the weather had gotten that particular memo, because the sky was overcast. She didn't mind getting wet in a swimsuit, but eating in the rain seemed damper than necessary.

"It's going to storm," she pointed out, just in case he hadn't noticed the clouds forming overhead.

He produced an umbrella. "Voilà."

"Wow. He brings food *and* he speaks French."

He rattled off a few phrases. The words sure sounded good, but he could have been reading her the French tax code for all she knew. "What did you say?"

His eyes warmed, getting that gleam she liked so much. The look that made her heat up, her girl parts jump up and down and go "Pick me!"

"Dirty French words I learned from a sailor. In alphabetical order."

"God. That's fabulous. Tell me more."

She stepped outside, shoving her feet into her sandals. Since "you busy?" hadn't spelled out the date-night possibilities, she'd opted for wearing a yellow-and-white-checkered sundress. The straps were tiny scraps of lace, more like a really nice picture frame for her boobs. She liked the way the full skirt felt swishing around her thighs, like a Southern belle.

"You look gorgeous," he said, his voice husky. Mission accomplished. He clearly liked her dress, too. Maybe, if she was lucky, he'd like her *out* of the dress even better. Smiling, she followed him.

He'd picked out the perfect spot for a picnic on the beach. Palm trees surrounding them, the surf beating gently on the shore and the moon shining over the water.

"You give good dates," she said softy.

He settled her on the sand on a blanket and popped the top on the basket. He'd brought champagne, which scored him immediate bonus points on her dating scorecard. He also had cold chicken, rolls, a chilled crème brûlée and strawberries. There were advantages to dating a chef.

She spooned up the last bit of her dessert. It was every bit as good as it had looked, and she must have made a noise.

Mason nudged her shoulder with his own. "Happy noise?"

"You bet." She eyed the remnants of their picnic ruefully. "You have to know you're an amazing cook."

"Practice," he said humbly.

"Where have you cooked?"

"Lots of places." He stared out at the ocean, and she'd bet he wasn't seeing the waves. "Do you cook?"

The last time she'd baked something from scratch had been…never. "I'm more of a cake-mix gal, although I do make a mean cake-tini."

In fact, a cake-tini was her all-time favorite drink. Who didn't like pineapple vodka and whipped cream?

He shuddered. "Cake mix doesn't count."

"Hey. If I want cake, I make cake. Duncan Hines and I are best friends."

"Tell me what you want," he said, watching her now and not the ocean. "And I'll get it for you."

"Cake?"

"That, too," he answered.

MASON WASN'T ROMANTIC. In fact, he was a resounding *hell no* in that particular department. He'd fought battles in all four corners of the world. He knew a dozen ways to kill a man with his bare hands. He'd spent two weeks in a foxhole, drinking his own piss when the water ran out because that was what it took to get the job done and bring his team home. Dating Maddie to someone else's script sucked.

Worse, it seemed to be working. Her eyes glowed as she grinned at him from the other side of their picnic blanket. She appeared to be enjoying herself, which made him want to smile himself. Instead, he filled her plastic champagne flute.

"It *is* Fantasy Island." Her mouth curved up in the prettiest smile. "You going to tell me a fantasy?"

Good thing he wasn't a drinking man, because *that* request made him choke.

"What do you know about fantasies?" Gray had explained the resort's kinky cocktail menu to the team, but Mason hadn't been entirely sure if he believed the

team leader. Was that how Gray and Laney had gotten together in the first place? Did hotel guests really use drink names as code for the sexual fantasies they wanted to act out? It seemed simpler just to ask outright, but people got uptight about what they liked, or thought other people would judge them. Frankly, he was too old to surprise. He'd also spent plenty of time propping up the wall in various bars around the world while he waited for his fellow SEALs to wrap up a night of drinking, and the drinks lists were fairly predictable. Blowjobs, cherries and virgins. He got why that appealed to a bar full of men, but why would Maddie be interested?

She sighed and knocked back half of her champagne.

"You need to loosen up," she informed him. "When's the last time you had fun?"

"I'm having fun right now," he pointed out.

"Oh." She blinked and held her glass out. "That's all right, then."

He knew how to have fun. True, he didn't do it like Levi, but he'd had plenty of good times. He topped off her glass, although he suspected she needed to go a little easier on the champagne. She snuggled into his side and he wrapped his arm around her, tugging her closer.

"Would you order off the drinks menu?"

He thought about that for a minute. "I'm not much of a drinker," he admitted. "Maybe I could play bartender in this fantasy of yours."

She stabbed him in the chest with a finger. "Not the *alcohol* menu. The sex menu."

He should check the alcohol content on that champagne. "You know about that?"

She shrugged. "Everyone knows about it. I'd heard rumors before I landed. You can't keep a thing like that secret. Point and pick."

"Is that what you're planning to do?" he asked hoarsely.

She set her glass in the stand, where it promptly fell over. "It doesn't seem like my kind of thing," she admitted. "It seems awkward. And what if the person you're ordering with likes something different? Or didn't realize you'd be asking?"

He met her gaze. "Ask me for anything."

Because in all honesty, he'd be happy to have sex with her under pretty much any circumstances. If she wanted to say "I'd like a *Long Slow Screw Against the Wall*" instead of "Take me to bed and fuck me, big boy"? Well, those were just words, and all he cared about was her intent. And giving her multiple orgasms.

"True." She wet her lips with her tongue, an expression of *something* on her face. He wasn't sure what that something was, but he could guess because he was feeling plenty of things himself. Things like need and lust and an intense desire to strip her clothes off her and lick the champagne from her mouth. From other places, too, if she was feeling adventurous. He might not be much of a drinker if his drink came in a glass, but a Maddie-shaped cup was one big *hell yeah*.

He planted his hands on the picnic blanket and leaned in. She didn't retreat. "Can I make you a drink?"

She breathed out unsteadily, the small puff of air teasing his mouth. Any closer and they'd be kissing. Kissing was good, but he really, really needed to hear her answer. She searched his face, as if he had a menu

printed there. He didn't know what she was choosing, but damn if he didn't hope it was him.

"Okay," she said, her eyes drifting closed, her body swaying closer. "But…"

"Tell me what your objections are and I'll fix them."

Her mouth brushed his. "I want a list of my options, okay?"

"Anything," he growled, and he meant it.

Her eyes popped open and she giggled. "You can't promise me that. What if I wanted to do something *really* kinky and you weren't okay with it?"

He couldn't imagine anything she'd want to do that he wouldn't. Maddie talked big, she lived to shock him and she definitely didn't filter her words, but he also got the sense that her experience wasn't as broad as she liked to pretend.

"Feel free to shock me," he added drily.

Another giggle. "You should have a safe word."

He shot her a glance and started packing up the picnic basket. "Is your drink called *Tie You Up*? Or *My Sweet Submissive*?"

She blew out a breath. "Now you're teasing."

Only partly, although his personal tastes didn't include ropes and whips.

"I'm all ears," he said instead and tugged her gently to her feet.

"I really want to say the right thing," she admitted, a slight hitch in her voice.

"There's no right or wrong answer, Maddie." And then, because she still looked uncertain and he'd never seen her hesitate, he said, "Do you read those magazine quiz thingies?"

"Like *Cosmo*? Sure. But if you do, you may have to surrender your man card."

He shrugged. "I have four sisters. You'd be amazed at how many magazine quizzes I've taken. They liked to use me as the male benchmark."

She grinned. "You took advantage of that, didn't you?"

"You bet. Otherwise I wouldn't have stood a chance. So here's a quiz for you," he continued, steering her up the beach and toward the guest villas. Wrapping an arm around her waist, he gave in to temptation and stroked his fingers over her hip. "You tell me which answer you'd have picked. You kiss your girl for the first time. After you break your lip-lock, you, A, tell her you've been fantasizing about kissing her for days—and that the reality is even better than the fantasy."

She leaned into him, her breast brushing against his arm. "Next option?"

"B, whisper that she's the hottest kisser ever—and you've got a list of other places you'd like to kiss her." If she couldn't think of places, well, he had a list just waiting on the tip of his tongue for her.

"Go on," she said breathlessly.

"Or C, praise her kissing skills and beg her to do it again just so you can be sure."

She sighed. "You make this hard."

"Give me more words." Unfortunately, his mind—and his dick—had precisely one interpretation of the word *hard* at the moment, and it was a very literal interpretation.

Her bungalow emerged out of the darkness. He should have walked slower.

She tugged on his hand. "Which would you have picked?"

"That's easy," he said smoothly. "D, all of the above."

"Wow. You're good." She fished in her bag for her key. Then she smiled up at him, biting her lower lip ever so slightly, and something in his chest turned over. "Come in?"

Taking her up on her offer made him feel guilty, but it didn't stop him from accepting. He kept a hand on the small of her back, steadying her when she tripped and launched herself at the door. Taking the key from her, he inserted it and opened the door.

"The bedroom's through that door. I'll be right back," she said and headed for the bathroom.

Six steps took him down the hallway to her bedroom, where a tornado must have touched down recently, because clothes were tossed everywhere. Maddie wasn't a tidy person. Apparently, she attacked getting dressed as gleefully as she did life. She also had awesome choices in panties. He stepped over the duvet that she'd wadded up and kicked to the floor. He'd bet she was as uninhibited in bed as she was licking whipped cream off his mouth.

Still, he didn't want to pressure her into anything. She had to make the call about tonight because, God, he was a bastard. He'd stolen her laptop and shadowed her every footstep for days—even if she didn't know it—and now he wanted to have sex with her? Yeah. Sign him up for the Asshole of the Month Club.

Maddie stepped into the room and his self-control problem was back just like that. It wasn't just that Maddie was pretty, or that he really liked her. Because she was damn gorgeous and he did. She was Maddie. Lik-

ing her was pretty much a given. But she didn't know he had an ulterior motive for asking her out, or that all this dating stuff wasn't him. He was just following a script written by a magazine writer, and the ability to carry out directions didn't make him worthy of having her.

"I should go," he said brusquely. *Off-limits*, he reminded himself.

"Stay." That was his Maddie. Blunt. Sexy. An unstoppable force of nature—although the champagne seemed to have put a dent in her ability to stand straight. She swayed a little and then pressed her palm against the wall to steady herself. She was cute when she was tipsy. Barefoot, she curled her toes into the hardwood, rocking backward as she stared at him, coming to some sort of decision. She'd painted her toenails bright red with little white daisies. That kind of decoration was hard to do, as he knew firsthand because his sisters had roped him into nail-painting duty more than once.

"Are you sure?"

"Two hundred percent." She blinked at him. "I could make it three hundred percent though, if you're feeling insecure."

"Tell me you're not drunk."

She blew him a kiss. "I shouldn't operate heavy machinery at the moment, but I'm not *that* tipsy. I'll even make up drink names if it makes you feel better."

"Yes." Damn it. He sounded hoarse and more than a little desperate.

"Oh, good." She launched herself at him. "I thought you'd never give it up."

9

Ladies, tonight's the night! That's all I'm going to say, other than: wish me luck! I'm a woman on a mission and Mr. Fantasy Fodder doesn't stand a chance. I'm ordering rose petals for the bed and a bottle of champagne (oh, all-inclusive resort! How I love thee!), plus I have what has to be the world's biggest box of condoms. I am wondering though, how you all handle the pressure of the Wedding Night. I want tonight to be absolutely perfect. I want to blow his mind and be the best lover he's ever had. Am I overthinking this? Underthinking it? I'm worried the main course will seem boring after all the fun appetizers. Help!

—MADDIE, Kiss and Tulle

"YOU SURE YOU want to play games with me?" Mason's gruff voice in her ear almost put the brakes on Maddie's pleasure. Almost, but not quite. Trying to get him into bed had been like racing an iceberg. She'd been getting nowhere fast, but now he wrapped his arms around her, one hand pulling her closer to his muscled

chest and the other cupping her butt, and that was a mighty fine answer. He wanted her. *He* definitely didn't want to let go. And that made her insides feel molten instead of icy, so maybe there was hope for that iceberg after all.

"You talk too much."

He stared down at her for a moment, all big, stern man, and then his mouth quirked up. "*You're* telling *me* that I talk too much?"

Picky beast. She slid her hand beneath his shirt. The man had muscles on his muscles, but the rest of him was smooth with just a sprinkling of hair. The pair of dog tags was a nice surprise, too. Winding the chain around her fingers, she tugged him into kissing distance.

Then she slid him a glance. "I'm officially saying, 'I told you so.'"

He spread his fingers over her butt, his fingertips grazing the crack. She was pretty sure they both felt the shiver that coursed through her. "About?"

"You're not just a chef. Or you've been a busy boy in a former life." She tugged on the metal tags around his neck, sifting the skin-warmed metal through her fingers. "Dog tags."

"Maybe they're decorative," he suggested, his non-answer more than enough answer for her. "Or maybe I've served a tour or two."

Imagining him as a soldier wasn't difficult. He had a watchful stillness about him, an awareness of his surroundings and an easy confidence in his body that she liked. "That's it? No details?" She ran her fingers over the dog tags.

"You want my biography?" His fingers stroked a

little deeper, fondling her butt and moving closer to wicked territory.

"That's an exit, not an entrance," she pointed out, but darn it, she sounded breathless.

"I thought you wanted to play games," he rasped, bending his head to whisper the words into her ear. He followed up with another wicked stroke.

"Yes, but I want to pick the game."

His hand squeezed, his finger moving. The thought of where they could take this sent pleasure streaking through her. She could feel his calluses on the sensitive skin, the pads of his fingers tracing the small dimples.

"If you pick tonight, do I get to pick tomorrow? In the spirit of being fair."

She could let him choose. She could give up control. He'd make it memorable and he'd absolutely make sure she came. He was kind of a gentleman like that.

"One night at a time."

"Chicken," he chided gently.

Probably. "I'm not a kinky sex expert," she warned.

His husky laugh said it all. "Do I look as if *I* am?"

He was big and rough around the edges. But also safe. She got the strong sense that the man lurking behind that hottie exterior was keeper material. If he was all tough badass on the outside, he was a sweet marshmallow on the inside.

"A gal can hope." And there was no time like the present to find out what he looked like naked, so she grabbed his hand and towed him into the bedroom. Not that he was putting up any resistance right now, but she'd worked too hard to get here to risk him bolting now. Mason had all these gentlemanly notions and she didn't need anything scaring him off.

"Strip," she ordered, throwing herself onto the bed. "Give me a show."

He arched a brow. "Just like that? I don't merit any foreplay?"

But his hands went to the edge of his T-shirt, fingering the cotton as another smile quirked at his mouth. She loved this looser, more fun side of Mason.

"Up." She waggled her fingers. "Make me a happy woman, okay?"

He shook his head, but pulled the shirt over his head in one swift move. Oh. Sooo worth waiting for. She considered making him put the shirt back on, just so she could unwrap her present again. Or make one of those animated GIFs of him. Fortunately, there was still plenty more to unwrap. If she was lucky, the rest of him would be just as cut.

"Now it's your turn." He didn't take his eyes off her as he folded his shirt neatly and set it over the back of a chair. Wow. The man was a closet neat freak? That didn't bode well for them. She shoved a silky kimono, a pair of sleep pants and tomorrow's clean thong off the bed, making room for him to sit down. She was... messy. And that was a generous estimate of her house-cleaning skills. Plus, the resort had been out of rose petals and the freebie champagne had yet to show up. Overall, her planning skills sucked.

"Who said this was a tit-for-tat relationship?"

"I could convince you." He dropped onto the bed, making short work of his boots and socks. She sighed happily. There was really nothing better than a man in just his blue jeans, and he deserved a reward for getting naked. In that spirit, she swung herself over his lap, setting her hands on his shoulders.

"Please do," she crooned, and he smiled slowly.

"Okay, then." He reached one hand up to cup the back of her neck and pulled her down to him for a kiss.

UNLIKE HIS, HER LIPS were soft and champagne flavored. She exhaled, rocking against him, riding his lap and his dick as though she was a cowgirl and he was her own personal stallion.

He deepened their kiss, licking the seam of her mouth, catching that breath. She stilled against him, as if she wanted to capture the sensation, drink it in and not miss a moment of it. Or maybe he was projecting because that simple kiss felt damned good. He did it again, licking deeper. She opened up for him on a gasp, her tongue brushing against his and then retreating in a wicked dance. He felt her shiver, her nails digging into his shoulders.

She kissed him back, her tongue exploring his lips and then his mouth. Heat surged through him, and suddenly playing fantasy games didn't seem like such a great idea. He wanted to be inside her, taking her deep, hearing her call his name as he thrust and she came. They could go slow the second time. Or tomorrow.

He kissed her more intimately, his tongue exploring her mouth thoroughly. When she moaned, he decided she really liked what they were doing. Thank God, because she'd tell him exactly what he was doing wrong, too, if she felt his kissing needed improvement or direction. His Maddie didn't hold back.

Her tongue tangled with his as she angled her head, trying to find a way to take him more, deeper, hell if he knew except it was raw and sloppy and the biggest turn-on ever. He'd be the best lover she ever had and then

maybe she'd give him another night. Another chance. And at least he kept his dumb-ass thoughts to himself as another bolt of pleasure seared through him.

When he finally broke their kiss, his breathing sounded ragged, but she got to him and he didn't mind her knowing. Not like she could miss the evidence pressing against her sweet pussy. Her mouth was slick and wet from his kiss, her lower lip trembling. She stared at him, a dazed look in her eyes, her breath catching.

"Do that again." She punctuated her order with another naughty wriggle.

"Happily," he growled, pulling her down for another kiss. His hands got busy, too, sliding her straps down. One good tug and her breasts popped free. That wasn't nearly enough, so he cradled her against his chest, pulling her dress and panties down and off, before falling back on the bed with her.

He definitely had her attention now, because she leaned up an elbow and grinned cheekily at him. "So, big guy, are we doing it missionary style?"

HE LOVED A good challenge, because he gave her another one of his slow, panty-melting grins. "Right. You prefer kinky."

She had a feeling she preferred *him*. Since he still had his jeans on, while she was buck naked, she reached down and popped his buttons, working her hand inside his boxers. If it was make-Maddie's-fantasies-come-true night, she knew exactly where she was starting. His penis butted against her palm and she fisted him, dragging her fingers slowly up the hard length. "This works for me."

He pulled away. That was the wrong direction. He was supposed to be moving *closer*, like get-inside-her close, not putting distance between them.

She squeezed his dick, running her fingers over the thick crown. "Stay put."

"I'm coming right back." He peeled her fingers off him, pressed a kiss against the tips and then tucked her hand against her pussy. "Think of something to do while I'm gone."

"I'm not waiting for you," she warned. "And you'd better come back naked." Kinky games were one thing. Walking away was definitely not on her list of sexy things.

He flashed her that quick grin of his. "Then I'll hurry."

"Masturbating's only sexy if you watch," she called after him as he disappeared into her hallway. She tried to listen for him, but the man moved like a stealth ninja. When he returned a few minutes later, he had a bowl in his hands. The contents rattled softly as he set it down. The good news was that he'd listened to her and lost his pants somewhere on his journey. And yeah, his penis was spectacular.

She levered up on her elbow, her hand falling away from her pussy as she stared at him. She'd rather have him than her fingers. "What's that for?"

"You're impatient. You know that, right?"

Ha. And he was an overachiever in the patience department. "Do you really care?"

In answer, he pulled an ice cube out of the bowl and drew it over her collarbone and down the slope of her chest. She didn't even try to hold back her shriek.

"Oh, my God, Mason, that's cold! You can't try everything you read about on the internet."

He didn't stop, just kept dragging that damned ice cube lower. "Shh. You're spoiling my game."

He touched her again, moving the ice cube lower. Honestly, she wasn't sure how she felt about this. It seemed kind of silly, really. And they were totally going to make a mess out of the sheets and the resort had one of those eco-friendly policies where they only changed things on request and… *Oh.* He circled her nipple with the ice cube and the tightening sensation shot straight to her clit. She'd had no idea there was any kind of connection there, but now the ice was an exquisite torment she couldn't get enough of. She pressed into his touch and he did it again, drawing a smaller circle this time. Okay. She could be convinced.

"Like that, don't you, sweetheart?"

"Mmm…more," she demanded.

He took orders well. He followed the ice cube with his mouth, his tongue exploring the skin he'd chilled. Heat. A tingling chill. A jolt shuddered through her as the erotic sensations washed over her. When his mouth closed over her nipple, sucking, she bit her lip at the raw feeling.

"I'm not cold anymore." If her words came out more moan than words, that was entirely Mason's fault.

"Good," he said hoarsely. "Let's see you how like this."

His devilish fingers, chilled from the ice cubes, slid through her folds. It was too much and not enough, a raw, erotic shock that had her arching up against him. Except…she wanted to touch him, too.

Go big and own it. She peeked in the bowl, hoping

for inspiration. And, hello, naughty idea. Not only had he brought ice, but he'd brought Popsicles. She'd had no idea her villa's kitchen was so well stocked. Or that Mason had such a creative imagination.

She grabbed a cherry Popsicle, which was definitely her new favorite flavor. At least her mouth wouldn't turn bright green or purple. Unless Mason had undisclosed alien sex fantasies, that wouldn't be a hot look.

"It's still my turn," he growled, still fingering her pussy.

"You bet." This was all about making him feel good after all. She eased the Popsicle into her mouth, pretending it was a certain part of Mason. Sure, the Popsicle was way too small and cold, but she worked it for all she was worth. Moving her mouth up and down the icy treat, swirling her tongue around the top. When it popped free with an audible sound, he groaned.

"You play dirty." He sounded approving.

Absolutely, and always in bed. Handing him the Popsicle, she reached for him, intending to go down on him. "Hold this and hold on. I've heard guys love this."

"Now that I've got this?" He waggled the Popsicle. "Nuh-uh. It's still my turn, sweetheart." He dropped down the bed, maneuvering his shoulders between her thighs, pushing her wide. She had just enough time to wonder what she looked like before something cold slicked over her pussy.

"Mason—"

"Shh. I'm working here." He parted her and then he ran the damned Popsicle around her clit. *Oh.* The shiver working up from her toes had absolutely, positively nothing to do with being cold, because she was hot all over.

MADDIE SHRIEKED SOMETHING. Mason couldn't tell what, didn't care, because her hands were pulling at his shoulders. The sounds she made were more erotic than the dirtiest words because she didn't hold back. This was his Maddie, letting him touch her.

He'd make this good for her. He'd make this fantasy come true, and then he'd find out what else she dreamed about and do that, too. Whatever she wanted, she got it.

He moved his mouth over the skin of her thigh. She tasted sweet, felt even softer, and the heat of her...the speed with which her Popsicle was melting pointed out the flaw in this plan of hers.

"Mason," she pleaded, her hips moving against his hands. More words followed his name, disjointed and throaty. He loved that he could make his smart, funny Maddie stop thinking and lose her train of thought.

Abandoning what remained of the Popsicle, he tossed it away. Maddie opened her mouth, but he didn't think she was about to criticize his lack of housekeeping skills. Just to be sure, however, he moved his mouth higher, closing the distance between him and her sweet spot. He licked her where she was cherry red, swiping his tongue up her slit. The icy cool of the Popsicle burst on his tongue, a bright hit of artificial flavor, followed by the taste of Maddie. And that taste? Absolutely exquisite.

He tipped her farther back onto the bed, cradling her hips with his hand. She sprawled on the mattress, her fingers pushing first into the sheets, and then fluttering to his shoulders. His head. Touching him in as many places as she could. Not good enough, not yet.

He went back to her cherry sweet spot and covered her with his mouth.

She shrieked his name, her hands grabbing on to his head and holding on. *Yeah. Just like that, sugar.*

Her legs fell open and he ate his sweet treat. Licked up her cream as he found her clit and pressed with his tongue. Flicked and rubbed as he pushed the tip of two fingers inside her slick channel. She shrieked some more—when she let go, she let go, which was just one more thing he loved about her.

Love.

Wait.

He froze for a moment and the chill sweeping him had nothing to do with ice or Popsicles, because that L-word wasn't supposed to pop into his head right now. Or *ever.* But her hands tugged on his head, her hips bucking against his face, and now wasn't the time to ask himself which it was, love or sex, because he could feel her thighs tensing, her heels digging into his back, and she was so close. Instead of thinking, he gave her more, sliding his fingers in, rubbing the pads of his fingertips against that one particular spot that makes her clench.

"Mason." His name. A breathy sigh this time. Funny how when she came, she got quiet, just letting go and coming undone in his arms like all the fireworks were on the inside now and required all her attention. And he had her, holding her tight until she finished and he could move up, pull her into his arms. Funny, too, how just this would be enough, making her feel good. Making her happy.

Fuck.

It really might be love after all.

MASON'S JAW CLENCHED as he pulled her into his arms. She was still humming, coming down from the most amazing orgasm high ever. Part of her had an immediate date with her pillow, and the mattress had never seemed softer, better, but she had *Mason* wrapped around her— and he had an erection that wouldn't quit. Wasting it would be a shame.

So she rolled onto her back, tugging him over her. He let her, settling easily between her hips. She wrapped her legs around his waist and it was just like before, except now he was kissing distance away. Knowing where his mouth had been got her hot. The wet slick of her juices on his lips was one of the most erotic sights she'd ever seen and she pressed her fingertips against his mouth.

This was probably the moment when she should say something witty or memorable—or at least apprecia- tive. Instead, she was more of a babbler and nonstop talker. She also gave directions, because there was no point in forgoing an orgasm just because her partner wasn't getting it right. But Mason was…Mason. And he wasn't like any of her other lovers. They were nice guys or—more often—bad boys, because if she was treating herself, she liked to do it right, with guys who knew how to make sure the night was fun. Mason was fun, too, but he was also something…*more*. If she hadn't still been quivering, her legs weak from the most in- credible orgasm she'd had in months or possibly for- ever, she would have taken a moment to think about it.

Instead, she ran her hands up his arms. He was sweat slicked, the muscles cording in the sexiest way as he held himself up over her.

Since it was her turn—and she really, really wanted

to feel him inside her sometime soon—she traced those delicious biceps with her hands. Followed with her mouth, leaning up to tongue his nipples. He groaned, a husky sound that was part curse, part her name.

"I'm right here," she said, as if there was any question of that.

Then he lowered his mouth, taking her. Their tongues tangled and all the games, the erotic refinements, didn't matter half as much as that raw connection. She tasted him. Licked him. Learning his mouth, his throat, the hard, ridged planes of his chest. His hands and mouth were equally busy, roaming over her curves, and his fingers found her pussy again. There was nothing fancy or sophisticated about this, just the exquisite heat of his touch and the need to press as much of her against as much of him as possible.

Eventually, he threw out an arm, reaching for the condoms on the bedside table. She was no help at all as he tore a packet open, because she was just waiting for him to put himself inside her. Or for her to take him. Right now, either worked for her as long as it happened now, now, *now*.

He dragged the tip down her slit and that was one more jolt of pleasure. His eyes were glazed, too, though, his breath coming in rough pants, and she pulled him closer so she could feel the tension and need vibrating through his big body. Whatever this was, whatever they were doing here in her bed, right now he was all hers.

He entered her slowly, inch by inch. And that felt so much better than his tongue or his fingers, filling up an empty place she hadn't realized she had. He paused when he was seated deep inside her.

"Okay?" He asked the question as if he was dead se-

rious, and she knew she should tell him that she didn't always need sweet and gentle. It was okay for him to *not* be a gentleman, to be just a little rough and let go all the way. He pulled out a few glorious, friction-filled inches, before pushing back inside her.

"Better than okay," she whispered, and then gave him a hint, drawing back and slamming back against him, forcing him deep and hard inside her body.

"Harder," he agreed, and then began a rough, satisfying rhythm that made her entire body hum with the pleasure of him. He drove in and she rose up to meet him, digging her fingernails into his shoulders as they pressed together. He pounded into her in a primal beat and the orgasm surprised her, coiling through her body in a burst of electric white. She wrapped arms and legs around him, burying her face in his collarbone as he pumped once more, twice, and then followed her over that glorious edge.

"Wow," she said, flopping back on her pillow. "That was amazing. *You're* amazing."

"You stole my line." He tucked an errant strand of hair behind her ear. He'd mussed her up good.

She grinned, a big, happy, wow-we-really-just-did-that smile that he wanted to see again today, tomorrow and fifty years from now. *Hell.*

"I'll wait while you come up with something," she murmured.

She'd be waiting awhile. It seemed she'd knocked all the words right out of his head. What they'd shared had been fantastic, mind-blowing and slightly kinky sex. If it had been any better, he'd be dead. He could

handle whatever she threw at him sexually. The adjectives? Not so much.

So instead, he draped an arm over her waist, just in case she had any thoughts of hopping out of bed and making a run for it. He never quite knew where he stood with Maddie. Maybe she'd change her mind about their vacation hookup.

About them.

Not that there was really a *them* since he was dating her under false pretenses, but the fantasy was an awesome one.

Running his fingers over the tattoo on her hip, he thought about the words she'd chosen to ink into her flesh. *More than a catbird.* He'd seen plenty of tattoos. It was practically obligatory to get one after a tour of duty, and this must have taken hours. It was a serious commitment. Since the last time he'd gotten her naked, reading hadn't been number one on his to-do list. He'd settled for admiring the delicate flowers swirling over her hip bone and around the ornate line of text. Nothing simple for her.

"You ever going to tell me the story behind your tattoo?"

She patted him sleepily on his chest. "You distract me when I'm naked."

He traced the words with his finger. "Spill."

"You're so sure there's a story?" she scoffed.

Yeah, he was, so he stayed silent. Sure enough, she sighed and kept on talking.

"It's part of an Ogden Nash poem," she said.

"I guess I should ask you who you were thinking of when you got your ink." Not that he really wanted to know. He'd rather run his fingers over her ink—over

her bare skin—instead of thinking about the other men who had undoubtedly shared her life.

"Myself," she said, surprising him. "There's no guy out there with a matching poem, if that's what you're asking."

He wanted to crush her against him, to give her another kiss. Hell, he was seconds away from volunteering to get ink with her, despite his dislike of needles.

"Why this poem?" He brushed his fingers over the words. They meant something to Maddie.

"The poem's about love," she said softly. "About loving more than other people hate. Ogden Nash was all in when it came to loving. I like that."

He should back off, should let go of his Maddie fantasies—because, whether she admitted it or not, that poem announced in indelible ink that she was holding out for love and forever, and he simply wasn't the man she thought he was. Hell, he wasn't even a real chef.

"Do you have to go?" Her fingers twisted in his dog tags.

"Not yet," he said, gazing down at her and tenderly stroking his thumb along her cheek. "But soon. I have an early-morning work call."

He knew he had to let go of her, no matter how impossible it seemed at the moment. One more kiss, one more night, he decided.

He'd never had a lover like Maddie, so willing to try anything. Possibly everything. There was shit you didn't do, didn't ask for. Shit you sure as hell didn't *expect*.

"Okay," she mumbled drowsily, already drifting off. Too much champagne, too much sex.

"Good night, sweetheart," he whispered, feathering

kisses against her hair. It was stupid, since she was already out, but he wanted to do it even if he had no idea why. She'd wanted sex and he'd given it to her. Emotions weren't supposed to be part of their date night, particularly when he hadn't been up-front with her. And it wasn't as if he was some big feelings expert. He'd only had the one lover, when he was just a kid, and she'd been his wife. He'd screwed that up.

Everything since then had been sex, but he hadn't been shooting for any kind of world record—or any kind of relationship. Sometimes, if he got a little too lonely or the woman was a little too pretty, he started to wonder what-if. He didn't have to wonder with Maddie. She was downright beautiful inside and out, and it was that *inside* part that made him regret not having met her under better circumstances, in a time and place where he wasn't shipping out and wedded to Uncle Sam.

Not that he minded his current circumstances, since he was curled around her naked body, right after she'd served up the orgasm of the century. Hell, part of him wanted to grab his cell phone, text the guys and ask if they could believe what had just happened. Which probably meant he should surrender his man card on the spot, but Maddie had been amazing. They'd been amazing *together*. Which would just make getting up and leaving her alone in bed that much harder.

Yeah. He was pretty much screwed, and not in the good way, either.

10

MADDIE OVERSLEPT, WHICH was Mason's fault. First he'd done all those crazy things with the Popsicle, then he'd loved her until she'd fallen asleep. She probably should have been embarrassed that he'd worn her out but, hey, it had been in the best possible way. She looked forward to doing it again.

Unfortunately, the man in question had slipped out at some ungodly hour. If she'd been back home, she'd have been just going to bed, and instead he was getting up. When she'd protested—and, admittedly, she hadn't been all that coherent because dark o'clock was her conversational nadir—he'd brushed a kiss over her forehead and said the magic incantation. *Work.*

So what if she already felt a gnawing ache at his absence and missed the feel of his warm, strong arms around her? *Don't be ridiculous. You have plenty of work yourself.* With her time on the island winding down, she needed to wrap up the rest of her blog entries. She'd covered the villas, the food and the romantic cocktails. Today was wedding day, except, when she finally woke up early in the afternoon, she had a

message from reception telling her that the Guzman party had canceled and wouldn't be getting married after all. Unfortunately, no other nuptials were scheduled for today or even for the rest of the week. Which meant she was SOL unless she could find some faux stand-ins.

The island was quiet and nearly deserted when she stepped outside. There was plenty of sun, though, so her shots would come out. Julieta had wanted a sunset ceremony and the day was perfect for that. She'd shot the other woman a quick sympathetic email. She didn't know what was up, but she hoped Julieta was okay and that Mr. Guzman hadn't broken up with her right before the wedding. Or maybe the bride-to-be had gotten cold feet, their private plane had broken down or any one of a dozen other reasons that still left Maddie in the lurch, looking for a replacement couple.

Unfortunately, she kept mentally casting Mason as the groom, which wasn't a good thing. He was like the fish she didn't get to keep and had to throw back. Sex with Mason had been out-of-this-world perfect. Who knew Fantasy Island could live up to its name? Or that her stoic chef would be so very, very good at role-playing? He made her feel like the center of his universe—that elusive, intangible something she'd craved watching other people's weddings. She'd never met a guy who would do anything for her, up to and including Mr. I'll-Buy-You-Lobster-And-Break-Up-With-You.

Things seemed different with Mason. *She* was different. Sure, the sex was awesome, but that wasn't all. He listened to her. And, underneath his tough-guy exterior, he was one big sweeter-than-candy marshmallow.

She trudged over to Ashley's villa and banged on the door. She needed a model, and Ashley was a pretty single girl. When her friend didn't answer right away, she banged again.

"Is there a fire?" Ashley pulled open the door, looking slightly disheveled. She wore a gray tank top and cotton shorts that revealed how seriously toned the woman was. She was also barefoot, her nails pink with white polka dots.

"Not yet. I need your help."

Ashley didn't hesitate. "Hit me."

"I need photographs of a beach wedding and my bride canceled on me."

Asking for favors sucked, but she *needed* these photos.

"You can say no," she rushed to say. "Participating is completely, one hundred percent optional."

Ashley nodded, and relief swept over Maddie. Her wedding would be a go. "Got it. What am I doing?"

"Getting hitched."

Ashley grinned. "I think you should give me a ring if you're going to pop the question. Since I doubt you're asking me, who am I marrying?" She looked down at her pajamas. "And do I get to change first?"

"Thank you." She babbled more words, shoving a plastic bag of clothing at Ashley. "The groom is TBD, but I'll have one for you. I promise.

Ashley peeked inside and grinned. "You owe me a drink. A good one."

Maddie figured the white string bikini with *BRIDE* sequined over the butt was worth an entire magnum of champagne, and Ashley hadn't even spotted the lacy

pareo yet. Plus, Maddie had a crown of flowers in a box and a Home Shopping Network wedding-band set.

"Meet me on the beach in fifteen minutes."

"Roger that." Ashley flashed her another grin and then disappeared back inside her bungalow, the bikini clutched in her fist. Now all she needed was a groom. She found her victim at the pool. The pool guy was stacking another one of his never-ending piles of towels. He'd do. She marched over and tapped him on the shoulder.

He swung around, an easy grin on his lips as she scanned his name tag. "Morning, darling."

He was big and buff, if slightly tired looking, and absolutely perfect. "I need to borrow you, Levi."

He grinned and ran a hand down his front. "Do I pass inspection?"

She gave him another assessing stare. "You'd be even better if you were blond, but otherwise you're perfect."

"First time I've heard that today," he muttered, the grin fading.

She'd empathize about the bad day later—when she wasn't losing the light. "So that's a *yes* on the borrow?"

He jammed the rest of the towels onto the shelf and turned around. "All yours. Lead on."

Maddie wasn't sure what he'd expected, but when she directed him onto the beach where Ashley was waiting, he cursed beneath his breath. Since Ashley was absolutely stunning, Maddie wasn't sure what the problem was. Ashley didn't seem particularly thrilled to see her faux groom, either.

"Hey, Maddie?"

"What's up?" If they didn't get started soon, she'd miss the sunset.

"What exactly am I doing here?"

"Getting married." She beamed at him and handed him a beach bag. "Your clothes are in there. Go change."

For a minute, it appeared Levi might drop his pants right there on the beach. Possibly, Maddie decided, because Ashley was glaring at him. Then, with a muttered curse, he disappeared into a grove of palm trees. Nice. She had a groom with a potty mouth. Thank God for fantasies—and Photoshop.

"You're cranky. Tell me why." She positioned Ashley on the sand and eyed the horizon. Ten minutes until sunset. She hoped Levi would hurry up, or she'd have to go drag him out here herself.

Ashley made a face. "Did you have to pick him?"

"I assure you, I had purely superficial reasons. He's hunky. He's tall. He's also the only single guy I could scare up who was bachelor-aged."

Ashley snorted. "His ego's even bigger than he is. I wouldn't marry him if he was the last man on earth."

"Right back at you, sunshine," Levi drawled, striding over to join them. He wore the pair of white swim trunks with *GROOM* embroidered on the butt that she'd picked out for the shoot from the hotel gift shop. The shorts rode low on his hips, the black band of his underwear peeking out. His steel-toes flopped untied around his ankles. How anyone wore those in the sand was beyond Maddie.

"I'm demanding hazard pay for this particular job," he grumbled, hiking up the shorts.

Ashley leaned over and smacked his butt. "Toe the line, buddy. And lose the boots. You look ridiculous."

While the two of them bickered over Levi's choice in footwear, Maddie waved over the male employee the resort had sent to stand in as the minister. Their minister was a dignified middle-aged man in a cream linen suit.

"Okay, guys. Let's get started."

While the minister began the ceremony, Maddie got busy with her camera. At some point, Ashley must have won the footwear war, because Levi was barefoot. At the minister's prompting, the two joined hands and Maddie clicked away. The shots would look gorgeous and her blog followers would eat it up.

"Maybe we should have discussed exclusivity," a deep voice growled in her ear. Hard arms snaked around her waist, pulling her back against a warm, familiar body. "What are you doing with poor Levi?"

"Nothing too permanent." She flashed a grin up at Mason. "I'm marrying him."

He bent his head and nipped her ear. "That was fast."

"To Ashley."

He grinned. "Even faster."

"Now that you're here, you can help," she said happily. Mason always made everything easier. "You can give the bride away. Just lose your shirt. We're going for the bare-chested-man edition."

"You just want to see me without my shirt."

"Added bonus and not part of my original plan. Scout's honor." She held up two fingers. "Chop, chop, because we're losing the light."

She started directing the pair, having Ashley walk down the rose-petal-strewn "aisle" that was a pretty stretch of white sand. Having obediently stripped off his shirt, Mason took her arm. He handed her over to Levi with an audible "Behave." Honestly, Maddie wasn't

sure which one he was talking to. There was a glint in Levi's eyes that promised mischief. She didn't know the man, but she recognized trouble when she saw it.

As the minister spoke, she moved around the trio, shooting.

"Good thing they're not doing this for real," Mason muttered as Ashley elbowed Levi in the ribs when he didn't add his "I do" fast enough. "Most of us aren't marriage material."

He could add her to that number. She could feel the heat of him behind her as he followed her easily, steadying her with his hands on her hips when she leaned in to capture a particularly tantalizing moment. At least Ashley and Levi had chemistry, even if they didn't have happily-ever-after in their future. She and Mason had that kind of spark, too, although without the animosity.

"You ever think about getting married?" she blurted, the words flying out of her mouth before she could take them back. Darn it. Now she probably sounded as if she was ring hungry. And it wasn't that. Not really. It was just that sometimes she was lonely and it would be nice to have someone around. Nicer still to wake up with that someone in the morning and go to bed with him at night after sharing the day's highs and lows. It was all too easy to imagine Mason being that guy.

On the other hand, she was pretty good at being on her own. Not having a permanent guy in her life meant she didn't have a chance to get lazy. She took care of herself.

"Are you proposing?" Dark eyes glinting, Mason wrapped his hands around her waist. "Because I'm definitely flattered. Hold on."

Before she could protest, he lifted her onto his shoulders so she could get some overhead shots. And holy wow…he didn't even have to strain to lift her over his head, and that was damned sexy because she wasn't tiny or small boned by any means. It took her a couple of moments to catch her breath. One minute, she had her feet on the ground and the next, her thighs were draped over his shoulders, his large, warm hands wrapped around her thighs as he steadied her. Her new position had other parts of her pressing against his neck as her dress billowed around her.

"Are you crazy?" she hissed at him. Damn it, he didn't even have enough hair to grab on to. She settled for digging her heels into his chest. The man was insane.

Are you proposing? His words echoed in her head, like some kind of crazy subliminal suggestion. Except it wasn't subliminal, was it? Not if she was thinking about it deliberately. He tucked her dress beneath her knee and patted it.

"You're good," he said, turning to point her toward the beach action. He did that a lot, made sure she had what she needed. He was such a sweet guy, and…just maybe he could be something else. Mason would take care of her, if she let him. It was a strangely seductive thought. He was big and safe, and clearly she could lean on him. Or sit on him. She patted his shoulder and snorted. He was strong enough to handle the pressure.

"I won't let you fall. Take your pictures," he said calmly. Ashley looked over and winked at her, and of course it was the perfect shot.

11

HE WAS 100 percent crazy. Watching his fellow SEAL fake marry Ashley Dixon made Mason fantasize. It was embarrassing but, since the daydreams were all in his head, he didn't have to admit the truth to anyone else. What if it was him and Maddie standing there, hand in hand on the beach, getting ready to tackle life together? *Whoa. Stand down, sailor.* Their relationship wasn't real—it was an illusion he was selling so he could play bodyguard on the down low. Their relationship wasn't any realer than the "marriage" happening in front of them.

Tick-tock, his internal clock reminded him. After Santiago was eliminated, Maddie wouldn't need a bodyguard, and SEAL Team Sigma had their extraction orders anyhow. He was almost out of time with her, which meant he needed to make every minute count.

"I now pronounce you man and wife." The minister announced the familiar words with a flourish and more than a hint of a Caribbean accent. "You may kiss the bride."

Uh-huh. Levi swooped before Ashley could take

defensive action, leaning her backward in a dramatic clinch. That kiss wasn't going to end well for Levi.

"Put me down." Maddie batted at Mason's shoulders, clearly determined to capture this particular angle up close. Given the way sparks usually flew between Levi and Ashley, she was right to hurry. Ashley would just as soon kill Levi as kiss him.

He swung her down and she headed straight for the "newlyweds," camera shutter clicking. He hoped she'd gotten her shots, because Ashley flipped Levi, landing the guy on his back in the sand. Levi grinned up at his "bride," clearly not bothered by his new position.

"My wife's into the rough stuff," he said to no one in particular.

"Funny," Ashley retorted, glowering down at him. Mason figured she was seconds away from kicking sand in Levi's face. Her "groom" must have come to the same conclusion, because he rolled, coming to his feet and throwing an arm around her.

"Smile for the camera, sunshine."

Ashley glared at Maddie, shrugging off Levi's hold. "Are we done here? Because I'm about to pull a Henry the Eighth and off my spouse."

Levi slouched off, grumbling. Somehow, he and Ashley couldn't stop quarreling and pushing each other's buttons. If Ashley continued to work with SEAL Team Sigma, they'd have to find a way to work it out. Maddie waved them off, then ambled over to a palm tree. She pulled herself up onto the trunk and started flipping through her photos. She looked windblown and happy. Sexy as hell. So, yeah, of course he had to go watch over her shoulder. Lean into her a little, so he could feel the warmth of her silky smooth leg pressing into his side.

Breathe in her soft floral scent. She rested an arm on his shoulder, as though she just accepted his presence. They fit together in a way he couldn't begin to explain.

She'd captured the expression on Levi's face perfectly. Hooyah. That SEAL was in trouble and didn't know it. Not that he was one to talk. The evening breeze played with the hem of Maddie's pretty sundress. The dress was made out of some kind of light, airy stuff. Now that he didn't have her thighs squeezing his head, he noticed that it was cream with polka dots. Better yet, she'd apparently opted to wear a red bra, the crimson color playing peekaboo with the thin fabric. Jesus. Did her panties match?

He needed a distraction stat. "I've discovered your secret. You have wedding fantasies."

She shrugged, as if it was no big deal. "Like I told you before, I like weddings."

Yeah. The whole blog thing made that clear. She leaned into him, watching his face. He wished he knew what she saw. "I could make you like them, too."

He snorted. "Small chance of that. I'm a guy. I've got genetic immunity."

"Mmm." She shot him a sidelong glance. "What about the garter dance? That's a wedding staple."

He nearly asked if she was offering to play show-and-tell. He and Bethany had run off for a Vegas wedding quickie, which meant certain parts of that weekend were a blur. He was pretty certain his bride had had one of those ruffly blue satin things tied around her upper thigh, but he'd also been eighteen and in a rush. A rush to get married, to ship out, to get busy living. He hadn't understood the appeal of slowing down and appreciating what he had.

"You don't have a garter." Just in the interest of fact-checking her statement, he smoothed his hand a little farther up her thigh, rubbing his thumb over all that silky, warm skin as he pushed her skirt higher.

"Can you toss me my bag?" She pointed to the canvas monstrosity dumped on the sand. He'd packed go bags with less stuff, he mused as he fetched it and handed it over to her. She rummaged inside and produced a candy necklace, one of those strings of pastel pink, blue and green candies his five-year-old niece adored.

"Now I've got the perfect accessory," she said coyly.

"You've got about a hundred calories," he countered.

"Uh-huh. Watch, big boy." She slid the necklace up over her bare foot. Okay. So maybe he could have a thing for tradition after all.

"Do you dance, too?" Could he get that lucky?

"I have to get it on first," she pointed out. "*Then* you can take it off."

She drew the necklace up over her knee, the beads bumping against his hand.

"I'm sensing a plan," he said, exhaling a slow, ragged breath. "And don't stop on my account. Keep right on going. It turns out that I may be a traditionalist after all."

"See? I told you you'd like weddings just fine."

Except for the vows and the happily-ever-after part, sure. The necklace wrapped around her thigh was sexy as hell.

Maybe he could handle weddings, as long as they involved Maddie.

And garters.

Yeah. He definitely liked the garter.

"I just remembered something." He stepped in closer, his shoulders pushing against her thighs. God bless palm trees that were the perfect height. "I'm supposed to remove that with my teeth."

YES. PLEASE.

And after Mason finished stripping her "garter" off? He could get started on her panties, because playful Mason was downright devastating. The man had a definite fun streak, but he kept it hidden from the rest of the world. Having the chance to see this side of him was like having the best of treasures. So if he wanted to play, she'd play.

She ran her hands up his arms. He was pure strength, the muscles in his arms corded and well defined. He hadn't put his shirt back on yet, either. Lucky her. "Of course, you don't like junk food, so I don't know if you can help me out here."

She, on the other hand, *loved* junk food. His dislike for sugar was a serious character flaw.

His eyes darkened as he stared at the sweet garter on her thigh. "I could make an exception."

She'd just bet he could. Without waiting for her answer, he wrapped a hand around her thigh. She wasn't a small woman, but he had big, manly hands and he made her feel delicate. That wasn't something she needed to feel, but a secret part of her liked it. More than she cared to admit.

"Remind me how this works," he said.

Happily. She covered his hand with her own, stroking the backs of his fingers. The rough warmth of his

callused digits sank into her, even better than the tropical sun. The beach was a pretty place and, better yet, they had it to themselves now. The minister had disappeared, and neither Levi nor Ashley had been interested in sticking around. They'd wandered off, still bickering.

"The garter used to be a fertility charm. All the guests would try to grab it, and the bride could end up trampled or in tatters."

"Brutal." A smile nudged his mouth as he rubbed his thumb over the bare skin of her thigh. He'd acquired new nicks and scratches since yesterday.

"So the bride started tossing her garter at the wedding party as a kind of red herring. They went after the garter and left her alone. Today, many women skip it. Or make it their 'something blue' and keep it under their dress."

He nodded solemnly. "So no sharing. That's good. I don't think I'd share well."

She braced her arms on the tree trunk. He wouldn't let her fall off, but temping gravity didn't seem prudent, either. "Some weddings, the best man removes it with his teeth."

"That sounds about right to me...but I promise not to bite hard." He slowly pushed up the hem of her dress. "Hold this."

She squeezed the fabric. Holy. Wow. This was going to be good. He lifted her legs, placing them on his shoulders.

"I think you're going to be a champion at this," she breathed, the whole world coming to a standstill around her.

He inhaled harshly as he got his first glimpse of

what she'd been hiding underneath her dress. Because yeah, she was definitely wearing date-night panties. The silky thong was fire-engine red.

"Surprise," she whispered. His head brushed her thigh, close enough that she could smell the scent of cinnamon and something tropical. He always smelled faintly of whatever he'd been cooking in that kitchen of his and, God help her, she loved cinnamon.

His lips moved up her thigh, his hands gently gripping her thighs.

"Relax," he said. "I won't let you fall."

Off the tree maybe, but who was going to stop her from falling for him? The necklace was inches from where she ached for him, but it might be too close to her heart, too.

He glanced up, as if he'd read her mind, his cheek resting on her bare thigh. The rough, sexy prickle of his stubble on her sensitive skin drove her crazy, but then he smiled at her, slow and sweet, and his words heated her up almost as much as his touch. Which was saying something, because just the small, soft stroke of his fingertips playing with the necklace had her melting.

"You're going to have to trust me, Maddie," he said. And waited.

Waited for her to decide, because he had to be the most patient man she'd ever met. Shoot. Were those tears prickling at her eyes? This was supposed to be a sexy game and…she was all in. She cupped his face in her hands.

"Okay. But just so we're clear? You let me fall and I kill you. And I get Ashley to help me. That girl has moves."

"So do I." He grinned at her once more before turning his face against her skin and *licking* her. Just a small touch, his tongue easing over the sensitive skin of her inner thigh in a sensual glide that had her sucking in a breath and tightening her grip on his shoulders. Her skirt billowed around his head and shoulders and there was no mistaking this for anything other than what it was. Sex on the beach. Just like the menu had promised.

He sucked on the tender skin and she groaned, hearing the telltale pop as the first candy bead on the necklace came free.

"They make panties like this." She was babbling, coming apart in a happy puddle of goo. She couldn't see his face, but, oh, God, she could feel him. Feel his tongue exploring her skin, his breath on her mound as he moved his head higher, the stubble on his jaw rasping against her.

He paused. "I'll add that to my shopping list."

So would she. His tongue made another foray, sweeping underneath the necklace and teasing higher. And it felt so good, so very, very good. Each new touch left her hotter and more shivery, impossibly aware of Mason. He exhaled and she felt it, right there where he wasn't touching yet but where he was headed. She wanted adventure and he'd give it to her in spades.

And he liked this, too. That was what got her even wetter, made it okay that she was perched like a princess on the palm tree, the rough bark digging into the thin satin of her panties. Palm trees weren't made for thongs, but she didn't have to be practical right now because she had Mason working magic between her thighs. He took his sweet time, though, and the lit-

tle gasps and sighs that she couldn't—wouldn't—hold back? Those didn't make him go faster at all. He was a man on a mission and she wanted to scream *mine* to the whole damned island.

He licked a delicious trail higher up her thigh, drawing sugary patterns against her skin. His thumbs pushed beneath the edge of her panties, his big hands cupping her butt, shielding her from the palm tree's rougher bits.

"I like this garter-dance business," he rasped, sounding like he meant every word.

"We're not dancing," she felt compelled to point out.

He exhaled and she felt *that*. "You're awfully literal for somebody who wants me to believe a candy necklace is a garter."

His thumb slid beneath the fabric of her panties in a bluntly erotic caress. Swept up her soaked folds, parting her, finding her clit and pressing. It was a good thing she was sitting down, because her legs wouldn't hold her now.

"You have an excellent imagination," she said.

"You have no idea," he growled. God. She loved it when he went all cranky, surly male on her. She had no idea what was going through his head, but he was thinking something and he wasn't indifferent.

"And *you're* stopping." There had to be a rule against leaving a gal hanging on a palm tree halfway to orgasm, and she'd invoke it.

"Complaints." But he said it with a roguish smile now, his thumb flicking and stroking her clit. Just that little bit of him was almost enough to send her over the edge. But she was playing a long game today and she wanted all of him. A quickie orgasm on the beach wasn't enough.

He lowered his head—slowly, which made her think that one of these days, before her vacation was over, she need to figure out what it took to make him lose control—and stroked his other thumb over the red satin.

"You're so pretty."

He made her feel like the most amazing woman he'd ever met, as if she was a fantasy lover who really, truly belonged on Fantasy Island. She was erotic and powerful. With Mason, she wasn't standing on the sidelines, watching others live out her secret dreams. He was everything she'd dreamed about, and it was funny that she'd met him here. What were the chances of that?

He eased her panties to the side, exposing her. "You're even sweeter here."

She wasn't sure what had happened to their garter dance, but she wasn't complaining. She was wet and aroused, aching for more of a touch he was more than willing to give her. He cupped her butt in his hands, angling her, supporting her, and then he lowered his mouth to her. Her whole body sang with the pleasure of it. He licked and suckled, his tongue pressing against her clit in a steady, knowing rhythm. Each perfectly timed stroke pushed her higher, her heels digging hard into his back as she rode his mouth with gleeful abandon.

When the pleasure inside her snapped, the orgasm rippling through her, he kissed her through that, too, easing her down, keeping her safe as she shrieked out his name and lost herself to the sensation.

Eventually she came back to herself and released her death grip on his head. He snapped the necklace free, fisting the tiny pieces of candy like a knight seizing his lady's favor, except there was nothing chaste about

how Mason had touched her. What he'd done was raw and erotic, and she wouldn't have had it any other way.

He slid up her body, his eyes never leaving her face. "I'm keeping the necklace."

He could keep whatever he wanted. "Are we done?"

"Not at all." He swept her up in his arms, snagging her bag.

"Oh, good." The ease with which he lifted her made her feel skinny and delicate. She wasn't those things—didn't mind that she wasn't because Mason clearly enjoyed her curves—but it was nice to be held so close. Plus, her knees were all quivery. He could go Neanderthal on her anytime he wanted.

He carried her back to the villa with long, easy strides, not saying anything in particular. She rested her face against his chest, drinking in the way his fingers caressed the bare skin of her back. Her big red-and-white Aztec-print bag bumped his mighty fine ass with each step he took, but he didn't look as though he minded, and if she got any more turned on, she'd spontaneously combust.

"No sex on the beach?" She had to ask.

A grin curved his mouth. "You'd sunburn."

"It's after sunset. Chicken." She grinned at him. God, he was cute.

He nipped her mouth in a quick, hard kiss, striding up the path. "I'm voting for a bed."

NORMALLY, MASON COULD keep his inner caveman in check, even if his imagination sometimes suggested other, fun ways to please his partner. Today? Not so much. He felt a primal satisfaction in holding Maddie

close, in carrying her. She wasn't getting away from him now.

Not that she looked as if she was trying.

She tugged at his shirt, licking the sensitive hollow of his collarbone before she sucked the skin. Pleasure followed the sharp, bright burst of pain. Jesus. She couldn't wait, either, and *that* definitely made his caveman happy.

He somehow got the door to her villa open, dumped her bag on the couch and slid the dead bolt home. A housekeeping interruption wasn't part of his plans.

"Bedroom," she panted, sliding her hands beneath his T-shirt.

God. She drove him crazy. The feel of her wet, lush mouth suckling him, that adorable curiosity of hers... that and her uninhibited hunger for him? Yeah. He was a total goner. He took her into the bedroom, shoving down the covers and dropping her onto the mattress. After setting his phone on the bedside table—although he'd kill Gray if their recall timeline got stepped up—he performed a mental weapons check. He was clear.

"Get naked." She popped up, hands tugging impatiently at his clothes. Her landing had tossed her skirt up around her waist, and her red thong was a thing of beauty. "Or I'm not waiting."

When she ran a finger over her satin-covered center, he almost exploded.

"You're waiting."

She licked her lips, a devilish smile lighting up her face. "Make me."

"Is that a dare, sweetheart?"

She reached for his belt, tugging and undoing him.

THE HUNGRY LOOK in Maddie's eyes was hot, and holding on was the last thing Mason wanted to do, but he had to make this good for her. He needed her to remember this, remember *them*. Bracing his body over hers, he planted his knees on either side of her hips and captured her hands in one of his. She didn't resist when he pulled them over her head and twisted her ponytail around his hand, tugging her head back to expose the soft curve of her throat. She was so close to him that there wasn't an inch of space left between them and yet she was nowhere near enough.

She tilted her hips, cradling his dick against hot, damp skin.

"I said wait," he growled, because if she kept sliding herself along the length of him, he *was* done for.

She rocked against him, pretty brown eyes meeting his as she smiled. Slowly. She knew exactly how to tease him. "And I said *now*."

"Maybe we should play a game." And just to make his point, to tease her back, he slid himself over the seam of her red thong. She felt so damned sexy, laid open beneath him and trusting him to make this good for them both. She twined her legs around his, meeting his next stroke with an erotic promise that worked a groan from him. *Killing him.*

"I've had my appetizer. Now it's time for the main course." She wrapped her legs around his hips, arching up against him in blatant demand.

"Pick out a drink," he said and she leaned up and bit his lower lip. Jesus.

"You passed on *Sex on the Beach*. I'm not sure you deserve another choice." She didn't move her hands, though.

"Try me." He didn't bother disguising the rough note to his voice. She got to him, undid him in the best possible way.

She paused a beat, but the delicate furrow between her brows said she was clearly thinking. Sort of. He gave her another long, slow glide, the heat of her searing him through her panties. "I'm not sure if I can come up with anything that's not completely pornographic."

Could you be any more perfect? "Pornographic works really well for me right now," he rumbled, meaning every word of it, and her smile got wider.

"Kiss on the Lips." She stared at him, challenge written all over her lovely face. Maddie had a mouth made for kissing, so he leaned down and covered her lips with his. He wasn't sure what came next in this game, had no damn clue if he was being honest, but being skin to skin with her answered some deep-seated need he hadn't even realized he had. She kissed him back, her soft, supple mouth devouring his as hungrily as he took hers. *Mine.* The possessive thought came out of nowhere, but it felt good, too. He accepted it, let it go for later as he lost himself in their kiss.

"That's good." She sounded breathless when he lifted his head, her heels rubbing against his back. "I think I deserve a reward, which means you should definitely get naked."

That sounded like a good plan. Letting go, he sat up and yanked his shirt over his head.

"Maybe you could make it a really, really big reward?" Her gaze slid to his belt. "And lose the pants?"

Perfectly happy to make *her* happy, he stood up and stripped off his boots and pants, before shoving his boxer briefs down his legs. When he looked up, she

still had her arms stretched over her head and she was raking her eyes over him appreciatively. "Do you have another drink for me?"

She licked her lower lip. *"Silk Panties."*

"Maddie." She was killing him.

"Take my dress off," she said huskily.

He groaned, not sure when he'd lost control of what was happening. Her dress was made out of some kind of silky material. She skimmed her hands down her arms, taking the straps with her. The bodice clung to her breasts through a miracle or some feat of feminine engineering he sure appreciated. Impatient, he tugged and the fabric began to slide down.

The strapless red half bra she wore matched her thong. It ended just above the soft rise of her belly and it had to be the prettiest thing he'd ever seen, his Maddie framed in red. He could have admired her for hours, but she'd given him permission to touch, and a good soldier knew how to take orders.

"Beautiful," he said roughly, filling his palms with her gorgeous curves. She gasped and wriggled, and he also knew how to take a hint. He cupped her through the satin, brushing her nipples with his thumbs as he tasted her skin, skimming his lips over her cleavage and learning every sensual inch of her.

Bringing her hands down, she started to work the hooks at the front with an endearing eagerness. There was no missing the aching desire in her gaze, or the way her brown eyes all but ate him up. She didn't hide the way she felt for him, and her openness was sexy as hell.

"Nuh-uh." He pulled her fingers away. "This is my present and I'm unwrapping it."

"The best way to open a Christmas present is by tearing the wrapping paper off," she protested, but she let him wrap her fingers around the headboard.

"Stay like that for me, sweetheart."

"Mason—" His name on her lips undid him. Full of need and heat—and the humor and life that was quintessentially Maddie. Her eyes danced as she watched him. Teased him some, because that was his Maddie. She *didn't* hold back. She was so damned irresistible, moving against him, trying to hurry him up when he planned on taking every minute, every hour she'd give him.

He pulled the sides of the bra apart, brushing his thumbs over her nipples before pulling the dress down her legs. She spread her legs wider, rocking against him.

"How much do you like those panties?"

"I'm happy to sacrifice to a good cause." Another wicked cant of her hips convinced him that waiting was overrated. Whatever she'd give him, he'd take.

He tore the panties off her, pushed his fingers into her wet folds and found heaven. She felt so damned good that he let out another groan because this welcome was all for him. He explored her with his fingers, tracing each fold, each sweet, sensitive spot until she was bucking against his hand, her fingers tightening on the headboard as her eyes closed and she rode his hand with complete abandon.

"Mason."

"Shh. I've got you," he promised. She let go, trusting him to make this good, and he'd die before he disappointed her. When she cried out, shattering in his arms, he pulled away briefly and fished the condom from his pant pocket.

Her eyes flew open. *"Now,"* she whispered. "No more excuses."

Hell yeah. He could do that. He pushed inside her with one smooth, hard stroke, not stopping until he had nothing more to give her. Pulled back and slammed forward, hot pleasure streaking through him.

"Again," she beseeched, her hips rising up to meet him. So he did it again. And then again and again, until she was shrieking his name, the headboard abandoned as she dug her nails into his back and hung on as if she really, really liked what he was doing.

Or liked him.

Yeah. That was good, because he liked *her* a whole hell of a lot, and her body pulled him closer, clenching, tightening as if she'd never let go, and it was perfect. Heaven, really. Fuck him, but he never wanted to be anywhere else but here with her and, when she came, chanting his name as if it was the passport to some magical happy place, he grinned like an idiot and followed her over the edge, right there with her.

After he'd pulled out and disposed of the condom, he wrapped his arms around her and gathered her close, breathing her in.

"Maddie?"

She muttered something, collapsing bonelessly against him, and he brushed a kiss over the top of her head, earning himself another wispy sigh. He, on the other hand, felt as if he could get up and run. Climb a mountain. Assault a beach or maybe two.

He pressed a second kiss against her hair, because why stop at one? "You were perfect."

"You'd be the perfect boyfriend if you'd just shut up," she mumbled.

"GIVE ME AN INCENTIVE," he said roughly, his mouth against her hair. "Make my night for me."

"My own day's been pretty perfect so far," she admitted.

Mason was…well, okay, he was perfect. The cherry on her awesome-day sundae and even better than dessert after a month of dieting. He wasn't in any rush, simply patient and *there*. She wanted that every day. Okay. She also wanted it every night, and just possibly every minute. Somehow hot vacation sex had become a relationship, and she definitely didn't want to lose him when their time together on Fantasy Island came to an end. But she didn't have to, did she?

She exhaled, and ran her hands up his bare chest. The holiday fling had been out of her comfort zone, and look how that had turned out. So she could do this, too.

"Marry me?" She smiled and grinned at him. *Live large. Be brave.* "Say *yes*."

She couldn't look away. She had to see his face, watch his reaction as he processed her impulsive question. A few days of getting to know Mason wasn't much compared to a lifetime of marriage, but she didn't need another year or ten to know Mason was one of a kind. He was bedrock and safety and a good guy, through and through. Fifty more dates wouldn't make her know him any better than she did now.

MASON HADN'T SEEN this coming.

So he had to ask. "Say that again?"

She stared at him as though he was speaking Greek, when he was the one clearly experiencing hearing loss,

but then she repeated her question. "Marry me? I know it's quick and we haven't known each other all that long, but when something's right, it's right. Right?" She frowned, her words picking up speed and tumbling out. "I love you."

Normally, he had some idea of what to say. He wasn't a dating virgin—wasn't any kind of virgin—and he had, after all, been married once, even if it hadn't worked out. Nothing, however, had prepared him for the look on Maddie's face. He had no idea how she managed to look both bold and tentative at the same time, but she did. He liked her a whole helluva lot. Maybe even *loved* her. But he'd been dating her under false pretenses and for a matter of days. He'd led beach assaults that had taken more time than they'd had together.

She plowed on though, clearly undeterred by his silence. Instead of waiting for him to say something— and he honestly had no idea how long it would be before his brain unfroze and started giving orders to his tongue again—she walked her fingers up his chest, stopping with her fingertips pressed against the spot between his ribs.

Then she opened her mouth and he knew he was finished. "I've got you in my heart, Mason Black, so I'm hoping you've got room for me right here in yours."

He didn't deserve a woman like her, and that was the truth.

"Maddie—" The hopeful look on her face about killed him. Damn it. She'd fallen in love with his cover story and she needed to know the truth. She wanted to marry him. She'd believed every word he'd given her, and now she thought he was her Mr. Perfect. Shame

flooded him. There were lines no man should cross, and he'd driven the emotional equivalent of a fucking Humvee over them.

"Maddie—" He said her name again, but finding words to come next was hard.

"Oh, my God." She froze on top of him, smile fading. "You're telling me *no*."

"It's not that." It was precisely that.

"Are you married? Am I an idiot? Of course I am."

That almost made him choke. "You're not an idiot." Because that honor went to him. How had he possibly thought any of this was a good idea? He'd had sex with her...and now look where that had gotten them.

Into bed and then into a huge heap of trouble.

His first response to her proposal was a *hell no*. He couldn't handle being married again. He could admit that to himself. As a SEAL, he'd trained to never accept less than his personal best from himself, and his first marriage had been an epic failure. He'd made promises to love and honor *forever*, but his forever had lasted a lousy eighteen months.

"It's me," he said, and her lips tightened. Now that he had his shock dialed back, her proposal was actually kind of sweet. Fantastic, too, if he was being honest.

Except he didn't do honesty, did he? Any more than he did marriage.

"Are you *trying* to check all the boxes in the breakup-speech-clichés list?" She stared down at him, her face a mask of embarrassment and hurt. She didn't move, though, and he wondered if she even knew her thighs were gripping his hips. She flushed angrily, her eyes taking on a wet sheen. He couldn't

tell if she was angry, sad or a combination of both. God. What if she cried?

"I'm not married," he said carefully, uncomfortably aware that he wasn't telling her the entire truth. Because if he was lucky enough to have a woman like Maddie as his own? There was no way in hell he'd cheat on her. "I'm divorced."

Maddie's mouth flew open, and he could practically hear her playing mental Ro Sham Bo to pick the first question to ask.

"I don't want to discuss Bethany," he said, right as his pager went off, recalling him to their base camp for immediate deployment. *Fuck.* Seriously? Uncle Sam had the worst timing ever. Surely whatever needed to be blown up or assaulted could have waited a couple of minutes more. "I have to go."

She glared down at him. "So that's it? That's the best you can do? I don't even merit the 'honey, I work for the CIA and now I have to go' excuse? Because it's actually okay to just say 'no, thank you' to a marriage proposal." Hitching in a breath, she swallowed hard. "In fact, the thank-you is entirely optional and could be replaced with something else."

Yeah. He had no problem imagining the alternatives running through her head. She shoved off him. Unfortunately, he should have shifted her off his dick before he told her the truth. While he sucked in a pained breath, she shot upright.

"I just proposed to you." She looked horrified. At least she didn't look as though she was going to cry anymore. And he…still had no idea what to say, not that she was waiting around for him to explain. She

bolted out of the bed, and that was his cue to get up and go to work. Her bed. Her heart.

Her rules.

12

I threw my first wedding yesterday! Okay, so it was more of a dress rehearsal, because no one was actually getting married, although I did score some awesome pics for you all. Mr. Fantasy Fodder came out to assist, seriously upping the hot-scenery quota while he helped set up the bridal arch. Weddings are a good look for him, and let's just say that the man knows his way around a palm tree...and he's a 12 out of 10 on the kissing scale. You all voted for *Sex on the Beach* in our last poll, and who says I can't take direction? I did my best to get busy on a palm tree, and let's just say that, while it was kinky awesomeness, our strategic retreat to the bedroom was a wise move. I've got palm-tree burn today!

—MADDIE, Kiss and Tulle

THE ENTIRE SEAL team had assembled on the beach by the time Mason reached base camp, geared up and ready for the Zodiac that would land in five minutes. It was a quick, rough ride out to the waiting Navy ves-

sel, and then they would board a Black Hawk and fly forty minutes inland to the jungle compound the Marcos brothers had built on the Belizean mainland. Which gave them approximately thirty minutes of ground time to get in, search for Santiago Marcos and get out. Not that he had anything or anyone to rush back to. Not anymore.

He had no business thinking about Maddie when he was on a mission, but she was stuck in his head and under his skin. Would she miss him? Sure, things had ended about as badly as they could, but he'd never worried about the people he left behind. He had his family back in California, but they had lives and families of their own. They'd miss him, mourn him, but he wasn't part of their everyday lives and they'd go on just fine without him. For that matter, so would Maddie. Maybe he'd been fooling himself, thinking what they had was love. He'd simply gotten caught up in the whole Fantasy Island thing and had turned a few days of sex into a relationship.

But, as stupid as it sounded even in the privacy of his head, this thing with Maddie *had* felt like a possibility. Not just a hookup, but a chance for something more. Clearly, she'd been thinking along the same lines, given the proposal that had come popping out of her mouth. And the stricken look on her face when he'd turned her down still gutted him. He'd hurt her when that was the last thing he'd wanted to do. But accepting was out of the question. Full-time relationships and SEALs didn't mix well, although he liked to think that his older self could handle things better than the eighteen-year-old kid he'd been. Of course, Maddie thought he was a chef. She had no idea he wasn't baking bread while she re-

covered from their marathon sex sessions. If she could see him now, face paint camouflaging his skin, geared up to assault a drug lord's jungle compound, she'd probably KO any *possibility* of the two of them taking things to the next level.

The Zodiac flew over the calm surface of the lagoon, coming in fast and hard. The nose ran up on the sand; the SEAL at the motor easing up just in time to avoid beaching. Spray kicked up as the boat came to a temporary halt.

Gray signaled the go and Mason joined the others in running across the sand. Levi ran like a damned gazelle and not like a man with fifty pounds of explosives strapped to his back. Lips peeled back, Levi's eyes lit up as his adrenaline started pumping. His buddy lived for this shit, and the chance to blow Santiago's hidey-hole up would be the cherry on the mission sundae. They piled in, grabbing on to pontoon lifelines as their driver reversed hard and took them out to sea.

Eight minutes later, they approached the waiting Navy vessel. The Black Hawk waiting on deck was their ride. Sigma Team would be one of two six-man squads. Gray had brought a replacement for Remy and, after a quick round of meet-and-greets, they piled into the chopper and lifted off. Once they were outbound, they went over the forecasts, running through the expected weather, sunrise and tide times.

Gray passed around a photo of Santiago for a double-check of their target and Mason committed the face to memory. Santiago's picture was followed by more pictures of known bodyguards and house servants. Like the rest of the team, he'd already memorized the descriptions of who did what. Santiago

wouldn't escape capture by pretending to be someone he wasn't, and the SEALs wouldn't accidentally take down the wrong man.

Levi eyed the approaching jungle cautiously. "You think they got snakes down there?"

Mason flicked him a glance. "You want me to lie to you? Or you want to just shoot anything that slithers?"

Levi shuddered. "I'll take that as a hell yeah. And yes, please."

"You got it." He peered out at the approaching compound. "Almost showtime."

Levi whistled. "Santiago's squatting in a goddamned palace."

The place did look pretty good. Since they were flying low, barely skimming the treetops to stay under any possible radar, their current view would have been a Realtor's wet dream. In the predawn light, the walls protecting Santiago's privacy were lit up with enough wattage to ensure no one got close without Santiago's guards spotting them. The house was two stories with lots of windows and wrought iron French balconies. The Marcos brothers hadn't skimped on the square footage, either, although jungle real estate probably came cheap. According to the plans Mason had reviewed, the mansion was eight thousand square feet. It had two pools, four guesthouses and a ten-car garage that housed a sweet collection of armor-plated Humvees. Cutting off Santiago's access to that particular escape route would be a pleasure.

The teams needed to get in and out quickly, because this op was happening without official sanction. The Belizean army didn't want to know what went down here, so this was a stealth operation.

"Status," Gray said into his headpiece. He listened briefly, then flashed the team a thumbs-up. "We're a go. Stand by."

The Black Hawk descended rapidly over the compound to the garage as the team moved into position. The bird had been modified to make a quiet descent. The crewman tossed the rope out of the open door. Gray went down the line first. After counting to three, Mason followed. The closer they went out the door, the faster they all made it to the ground. Grabbing the rope between his gloved hands and boots, he rode it down like a firehouse pole, the soles of his feet inches above Gray's head. The only thing standing between him and a brutal ground landing was his ability to hang on.

The next three men would be right behind them, moving equally fast because they'd be vulnerable to small-arms fire and Santiago's security while they were on the rope. The rope spun through his gloved hands as the chopper moved slowly forward, dragging the rope. Gray dropped away. Mason counted to two and then let go. The impact vibrated through his body, but he was already weapons up. Ten seconds later, drop complete, the entire team advanced toward the mansion. The house was still quiet. The second squad fanned out to cover the exit points with a 360-degree security perimeter. If Santiago tried to make a run for it, they'd hit him hard.

Levi dropped away to play with his gadgets. He'd rig the garage to blow, the explosion providing a useful decoy. And fun. Blowing stuff up was always satisfying, and Santiago hadn't earned the toys he had parked inside the garage.

Levi popped out of the shadows, moving lighter. "Five minutes to boom time."

"Move in," Gray ordered. "Let's go find our boy."

Breaching the compound was the work of seconds. The front door wasn't locked—stupid bastard—and there were plenty of first-floor windows. The two body-guards by the front door went down almost silently, clearly not expecting company. Muzzle up, Mason stepped inside behind Gray, sweeping the area with the barrel of his M4.

The plan called for them to sweep the house room by room and secure it. With the first two guards down, the entry was clear. Diego and Santiago lived like kings. Marble tiles lined the palatial entryway beneath a crystal chandelier like one he'd seen in the Liberace Museum in Vegas. He'd bought his mom a little version to hang over her dining room table. She'd have liked this one.

Gray motioned and they took the stairs. Gunfire erupted right as the garage went, the shock wave rocking the larger building. The chandelier bit the ground in an explosion of crystals. Good thing they hadn't been standing there. Mason made a mental note to earthquake-proof his mom's piece. Gray signaled for Levi and Mason to cover the left, and he and Sam moved toward the bedroom on the right.

According to the building plans, the bedrooms were located on the second level. Better yet, the first door they busted open turned out to be the mother lode. Not only was the room full, but the lights were on as the occupants reacted to the sound of gunfire and the explosions.

And…damn it. "We've got nonthreats," he said in low tones into his mouthpiece. Muzzle up, he stepped inside and surveyed. Two women and four—no, five— kids. He'd almost missed the little girl hiding under the table. The minute he and Levi came in, the kids started crying and one of the females came out swinging. Maybe she thought they'd go for the kids, but that was a line he'd never crossed and never would. Mason subdued her, pinning her arms behind her and whipping out his zip ties. *"Cálmate,"* he growled against her ear. *"No quiero hacerte daño."*

Or maybe she was a decoy, because Santiago sprinted away toward a door on the far side of the room. Shit. Nice for Santiago that he inspired such loyalty, but a pain in the ass for Mason.

"We've got eyes on Santiago," he barked. "Get in here double-time."

"I've got him," Levi growled, already moving. "Show me your hands. *Arrondilese y ponga sus manos en la cabeza.*"

Levi's move left Mason with seven noncombatants. Go him. Levi got to have all the fun. He kept his eyes on their hands. A five-year-old boy usually wasn't a threat, but the best way to stay alive was to assume everything would go wrong. Maybe Santiago left firearms lying around. Maybe he'd taught Santiago Junior to shoot. Mason had also been fired on before by women—and by men dressed as women. So there was no way to know for sure who was friendly and who was simply in the wrong place at the wrong time.

Now that he had the first nonthreat zip-tied and down on the ground, the rest followed. He hated mak-

ing little kids show their hands, but he'd seen good men shot by making assumptions. Who knew what Santiago and Diego had taught these little guys? Maddie's face flashed through his head, and he knew what she'd think. This was the part of the job that sucked.

Across the room, Levi barked out more Spanish and then, when Santiago failed to comply, cursed. "You've got five seconds to drop the gun."

Naturally, the guy raised the gun.

"Hooyah," Levi said, sounding downright pleasant. "Rules of engagement say I get to plug your ass with my bullet, seeing as how I feel threatened. I'll take Spanish lessons later and explain my feelings to you when you're in US custody."

Right. Time to take care of business. Turning his M4 toward Santiago, Mason squeezed off a round with surgical precision. The bullet smashed into the other man's wrist.

"You took my turn." Levi stepped over and kicked the gun away as Santiago alternated between cursing and bellowing in pain.

"You were taking too long," Mason bit out. "Get him up."

"You're a lucky bastard." Levi hauled Santiago to his feet, clipping his wrists behind him with a pair of plastic cuffs. "We brought our very own medic with us. Ask nicely, and he'll share the Band-Aids with you."

Mason swept the room one more time, but the non-threats had wisely decided to stand down and leave this to Santiago. He flicked on the lights and eyeballed the man Levi frog-marched over to him. Damn it.

"This isn't Santiago," he said. "I wish I could tell

you we've got our target, but we've got the wrong guy. Looks like him, and I'd lay money on a shared family tree, but we just struck out."

Levi cursed and barked commands into his headset, pushing Not Santiago toward the door. Two minutes later, they were back in the front hallway playing show-and-tell with the rest of the team.

"Bloody hell," Gray roared, before launching into a volley of Spanish. Their prisoner shook his head violently, firing back a few answers of his own.

"Santiago left an hour ago," Gray said. "This one claims to be the cousin. Since he's parked in Santiago's bedroom, cozied up with Santiago's wife and kids, he's either the decoy or a good liar."

Levi's fingers tightened on the man's collar. "Then, we'll take him along with us, just in case we're looking at option B and a surgery job."

Gray nodded. It wasn't unheard of for the drug traffickers to pay a visit to a plastic surgeon and get themselves a new face. It certainly made Mason's job harder, because how did you ID someone who looked nothing like his photos anymore? He suspected that wasn't the case here, but they'd take the presumably fake Santiago along with them and let someone else check him out.

Sam popped his head out of a side room. "House is clear, but you all might want to take a look at this."

Gray turned to the imposter and barked a question. For a moment, Mason thought the guy might not talk, but then he shrugged as if the answer wasn't a state secret. *"Es la oficina del jefe."*

After turning the perp over to two SEALs from the other unit for transport, Mason, Gray and Levi followed

Sam. The dude was generally Mr. Levelheaded—maybe it was all that medical training—and unfortunately, he hadn't been wrong. Nope. What was *wrong* was the contents of the small study. Not only had someone been watching everything that transpired on Fantasy Island through two video feeds of the main beach and the pier, but that someone had also been diligently surfing the internet and reading Maddie's blog. And blowing up pictures of her.

Mason fought to keep his emotions under control. Right now it didn't matter that he wanted to rip the watcher's throat out for stalking Maddie. What mattered was finding the guy—*fast*—and making sure he was in no condition to do it again.

"You think this stuff belongs to Santiago or Diego?" Gray asked, grabbing the computer tower.

Good plan. What they were looking at was probably the tip of the iceberg, and maybe one of the computer techs could learn more.

Mason rifled through a stack of printouts on the desktop. The dates on the bottom were from yesterday and today. "Diego was already in custody when these were run," he pointed out. "Makes it more likely to be Santiago's work."

"Whoever it is, he's sick, you got me?" Levi shook his head, taking in the monitors and then the pictures briefly, before he started yanking cords and separating the stuff into four piles. "He's got a real thing for your Maddie."

"He touches her, he dies." Which meant locating the guy stat.

"Not our call," Gray cautioned him. "You follow orders."

"And if we were looking at photos of Laney, you'd be the first to shoot."

Gray nodded tersely. "I'm planning on sticking around for her, though, so I'd remember that *not* following orders tends to lead to unpleasant crap like a court martial."

Duly noted. Unfortunately, shooting Santiago might not even be an option. The man was the king of escapes. He was always armed with an assault rifle and he'd spent the past two years in virtual lockdown in the jungles of Belize, hiding out in his fortified palace. No reckless spending, car racing or nightclubs for Santiago. Sure, they knew where he was more or less, but a single dirt road led to the guy's front door and the Black Hawks echoed. Today, despite their best efforts, he'd either seen or heard them coming and he'd cleared out.

Gray cursed, conducting a last visual sweep of the office. They practically qualified as professional movers, Mason decided. The place was neat—just a whole lot emptier than when they'd entered. Santiago could bitch to the US government if he didn't like his redecorating job. "If he's not here, where did he go?"

"Three guesses. The first two don't count." Mason grabbed his load of hardware. Seriously, he didn't want the souvenirs. Nope. What he wanted was action. The faster he got back to the Black Hawk, the faster they put the bird up in the air and made for Fantasy Island.

"Why would Santiago head for Fantasy Island? So what if he's got a picture fetish for Maddie? Doesn't mean he's going to risk it all to meet her in person."

Sam didn't hesitate, though. He hefted his pile of gear and hotfooted it out of the room.

"Because he believes he's uncatchable," Gray said grimly. "The man's an escape expert and a pain-in-the-ass Houdini. He's wriggled out of more tight spots than anyone else. Plus, the Fantasy Island wedding was a cover. It was going to be a high-level meeting of key players in the Marcos organization. A chance to party and spend some of the hundreds of millions they've made in the illegal drug trade." He blew out a breath. "Our boy likes his fiestas, and instead of a party, he got a re-org. Marcos is down for the count, so Santiago moves up to the number one spot."

Levi whistled. "You really think he's going after Maddie?"

"It's not a chance I'm taking." Mason picked up the pace, running through the front door and out into the courtyard.

Boots hit the ground next to him. "Not your call," Gray bit out.

"Seriously? You're going to give me shit on this one?" Because leaving Maddie alone and vulnerable wasn't happening. He'd left her alone in her room, sure, but he'd believed she was *safe*. That nothing bad could happen to her where she was.

Gray pulled ahead, tossing his armload of computer drives at the SEAL waiting inside the Black Hawk's empty bay. "No," he said solemnly. "I'm not. We'll let the other team take our bonus boy for a little Q and A. We'll go back to Fantasy Island."

"Quickly." Mason knew he'd catch hell for this one later, but he didn't give a shit. Passing over his load, he climbed on board, Sam and Levi on his heels.

"I wasn't proposing we stop and hit the duty-free," Gray said drily.

Jokes weren't cutting it right now. Mason wanted speed. "Santiago has a two-hour head start on us."

"And we've got a Black Hawk, the US military and a roomful of DEA tech geeks." Gray held up his phone. "DEA had been reporting plenty of chatter since Marcos went down. Santiago usually runs on radio silence—no email, no phone calls, no contact. His guys don't talk to him directly, but they know what the boss wants them to do. Cut the head off the organization and the lieutenants still need to talk, right? Santiago's boys are going to be itchy and looking for orders."

Levi cracked a hard smile. "So has ET phoned home yet?"

Gray nodded. "Looks like it. The DEA has been monitoring all of the phone lines and email accounts associated with known traffickers in Santiago's network, waiting for someone to make a move. We didn't have so much as a tickle this morning, but someone started making calls an hour ago. Santiago's on the move, he's pissed and he's looking to 'make a statement.'"

Mason's skin tightened, awareness prickling over him. He didn't need Gray's air quotes to tell him that the "statement" in question could be Maddie. The chopper blades started up, drowning out all other sound as the bird got airborne. Maddie was supposed to stay safe. She hadn't asked to be drawn into an international drug operation, and she had no idea that she was now the finish line in a race between a SEAL unit and a drug trafficker. He didn't want her to feel threatened or scared. He'd keep her safe, get her through this and

then he'd bug out like he should have done from the beginning. A woman like Maddie deserved a hell of a lot more than a man like him.

13

Hurry. Hurry. Hurry.

No. Turn the emotions off, let the training take over. Mason couldn't afford to miss anything, and rushing could be fatal. Never mind that the moment the Black Hawk touched down on the naval aircraft carrier cruising Belizean waters, he was itching to move. Swimming to shore seemed like the better option, but he'd wait for the Zodiac like a good little SEAL.

"Gave Ashley a heads-up." Gray prowled toward the railing that Mason was haunting. "She's armed." A statement of fact. "If Santiago did come back here and somehow beat us, Ashley's got your girl's back."

There was no point in pretending protecting Maddie wasn't personal, so Mason nodded sharply. "I hear you."

"Since there's a credible threat, we'll take her to a military base until we've found Santiago. We've got leads on the man. Cell phone and email chatter. That kind of stuff."

"Santiago's mine." He'd enjoy taking the drug trafficker apart piece by piece. Those photos of Maddie

had been creepy as hell, and the man needed to go down, fast and hard. No way Mason allowed the other man to get anywhere near Maddie.

Gray gave him a hard look. "We've got other orders. We pack up here; we ship out. Do *not* go vigilante on me."

"Copy that," he agreed, but they both knew he'd do whatever it took to keep Maddie safe. Gray would have felt the same way if it had been his woman in danger. No one hurt Laney on Gray's watch.

Ten minutes later, they were in the Zodiac and gunning for Fantasy Island. As the sailor brought them in, focusing with laser-like precision on the small break in the reef, Mason kept his own eyes trained on the shore. If Santiago had made it here first, he could be laid up in the jungle, waiting to open fire, or he could be making his way to Maddie's place. The island seemed as serene as ever, although a boatload of armed SEALs wasn't going to help the look any. Mason had to hope no one was watching, or they'd attribute an inflatable full of armed men to the Belizean navy, but waiting until dark wasn't an option.

As soon as the Zodiac hit the beach, he vaulted over the side, boots hitting the water hard. He'd get under cover. Fan out and head straight for Maddie. Gray's hand on his arm pulled him to a halt. *Not good.*

"Get Maddie and bring her back down to the beach. We roll in an hour."

"On it." There must have been something in his eyes—something he didn't want to examine too closely himself—because Gray nodded and let him go. Mason didn't waste time, either, heading straight for Maddie's villa at a dead run. Ashley would be undercover, eyes

on Maddie, so Mason went around back. If Santiago showed up, she'd trigger the alarm.

Breaking in through the bathroom was too easy. The villa had one of those exotic outdoor bathrooms, and it took mere seconds to hoist himself over the wall and drop down into her shower. The damned door didn't even lock—he just eased it to the side and he was in.

The bathroom looked as if it had been hit by a Category Three storm. Lingerie, dresses, flip-flops and a million teeny bottles of stuff were scattered everywhere. He paused. Listened. *Clear.* Cracking the door, he swept the room visually.

Maddie was asleep on the bed. Probably not on purpose, since she still had her laptop with its hot pink cover parked on her lap. Her head had fallen back, red hair fanning out over her pillow, a little whuff that was an almost snore escaping her. The sound would have been cute as hell if he hadn't been scanning the room for possible intruders.

Holding the gun down at his side, he moved swiftly to the bed. Sleeping Beauty needed to wake up and get with the let's-get-rescued program. Gently but firmly he covered her mouth with his hand, leaning down to whisper against her ear.

"Wake up, sweetheart."

THE HAND OVER her mouth woke Maddie up, the unexpected contact followed by the shock of a body pressed against her startling her when she'd gone to bed alone. She lived through a moment of sickening, adrenaline-laced panic before she realized who exactly was holding her.

"It's Mason," he growled unnecessarily. "No noise, okay? Nod your head for me if you understand."

Something wasn't right. *That* was what she understood, but she nodded, because, hello? The whole hand-over-the-mouth thing wasn't her kind of kink. And if it *wasn't* kink, she had a bigger problem. Besides, while it was clearly Mason looming over her, Mason who'd come uninvited into her room, he wasn't *her* Mason. He looked different, *harder*, and it wasn't just the black and green paint streaking his face.

"Is this some kind of game?" She tossed her laptop to the side, rolling instinctively away from him. "Because I think we already said everything we needed to say."

"We have to go," he whispered, not looking at her. Instead, he scanned the corners of her villa as if he expected something. "We need to get you off the island."

"I believe I said, 'Let's have a future together!' And you said, 'Over my dead body!' Or something way too close to that. You may have dressed it up with the 'it's not you, it's me' and the 'I'm not looking for a relationship right now' speeches, but that's what I heard."

"Look at me," he demanded, his harsh gaze swinging back to her face.

Oh, she was looking, all right—and nothing added up. This wasn't paintball attire, and something was seriously wrong. A noise outside the villa interrupted her crazy thoughts. She wasn't sure what it was—housekeeping cart, falling coconut, demented parrot—but Mason pulled some ninja stealth move, rolling her off the bed and beneath him. His hand came back over her mouth, his body tensing as he raised his weapon at her door. His *weapon*. Holy shit. He had a gun. He braced his free hand above

her head, his fingers curled around the stock, where she could see dirt and a smear of something red. Blood?

"Mason—" She jumped, suddenly afraid, her lungs closing up. Who *was* he?

"Shh," he whispered roughly against her hair. "Breathe for me. Let's see if we've got company."

She hadn't thought her heart could beat triple time, unless she was in heart-attack territory, but the sensation of his large, familiar-and-yet-not body pressing her down into the floor had her all but hyperventilating.

Dark brown eyes stared intently into hers. "Can you stay put for me? Do you need your inhaler?"

He had a *gun*. She'd agree to anything. When she nodded, he rolled off her and headed for the front of the villa. That worked for her. She lunged for the bedside phone. He froze, head swinging toward her, but the business end of the gun didn't budge from her front door.

"Don't," he warned, as if he was used to giving orders and being obeyed. Too bad for him that requests from madmen didn't count. Lifting the receiver off the base, she punched the button for security. Nothing. *Nada*. Not a dial tone, not a friendly voice.

He strode toward her, his face hard and closed off as he took in her panic and her finger banging away on the button for security. "Grab your purse. Your passport. Anything critical that you need that fits in a small bag."

Hell. No.

"Who are you?" she asked in a strangled voice. Did the bathroom door have a lock? Could she beat him there? "And don't give me the line about the chef again. If you're a chef, you're bat-shit crazy."

"I'm a US Navy SEAL," he growled. "Cut me some

slack here. I can't go into details, but I'm here on an op and there's a credible threat against you. We need to move you somewhere safe."

"If you're going to sell me a bridge next, I'm not buying."

Naturally, he advanced. *Back down* wasn't part of Mason Whoever-He-Was's vocabulary, any more than *concede* was in hers. She flung up a hand.

"Stop right there," she ordered.

He laughed. A harsh, guttural, grunting sound, but the bastard *laughed* at her.

"Maddie—"

She snarled at him and he actually backed up a step. "Yesterday I apparently proposed marriage to a total stranger. I'd like to recover from my humiliation alone, please."

"I'm not the guy for you, and we don't have time for this."

She met his gaze head-on. That was his Maddie. Leap first, look later and live large. "Believe me, we're in complete agreement there."

"I had a job to do," he stressed. "A *covert* job. I'm under orders not to tell anyone why I'm here."

"Uh-huh." She gestured toward him. "Let's say I agree to believe you about the whole secret-SEAL-mission thing, since your show-and-tell exhibit is fairly convincing. Does that mean you were under orders to sleep with me, too? As part of the whole 'undercover' deal?"

His face must have given him away, because she looked stunned. Being Maddie, however, it was only a temporary condition and she sprang into action.

"Oh, my God." She smacked him against the chest. "You *were*. What kind of military do we have these days? Does Uncle Sam pimp out his boys?"

"It wasn't like that." Not exactly. "You shot footage of our mission. I needed to make sure you didn't have any other videos or photos."

"So you're not Mr. Perfect. You're an undercover SEAL. And you…slept with me so you could check out my photos? Was it worth it?"

"I can explain," Mason said, even though he was pretty certain there was no way he could. Being the perfect boyfriend definitely didn't include lies of omission.

"Whoa. Stop right there." She held up a hand. "You're a US Navy SEAL. You're here on a job." She folded down two fingers on her other hand. "You had designs on my data." She folded down her pinkie. "And you let me think you wanted to date me because it was part of some supersecret military plan to make the world a better place?" She folded down her fourth finger and flashed him the bird. "That's what I think of that plan, *soldier*."

Her body vibrated with anger, but she wasn't an angel in this scenario, either. She'd come on to him first, even if he hadn't resisted. So they weren't done. *He* wasn't done. She could damn well listen to the rest of what he had to say.

"Now that you've gone all judge and jury on my ass, let's get a couple of things clear."

He leaned into her, bracing his arms on either side of her so that she had nowhere to go. Not that *that* stopped Maddie. She tried to duck under his arm, eyeing the

door as though she thought running would solve her problems. "I'm done talking with you."

He shifted, keeping her caged. "You're not talking *with* me. You're talking *at* me. Now it's my turn." She opened her mouth, clearly ready to argue some more with him. Too bad. "Nope." He laid the palm of his hand over her mouth. "My turn, not yours."

When her eyes narrowed, he added, "Bite me and it will be my turn for the next week."

"You suck," she mumbled. "I want to make that very clear."

True, but he still had something to say and she was going to listen.

"I had a job to do, a job that mattered. I can't give you details about why we're here. We have a credible threat on your person and we're moving you for your own safety." He felt her inhale. Teeth were coming. Or a knee to the balls. He deserved both, but didn't he also deserve some kind of understanding?

"Maybe you feel I should have been up front with you from the beginning," he continued. "I would have liked that, but it wasn't my call. I had three options. Option one—I just take your laptop and your stuff. You don't get it back. I have my team go through it and to hell with what happens to your data or your own job here on Fantasy Island. I find out what I need while you run around the island trying to figure out who stole your gear.

"Option two—I let US Customs do the same thing when you head back to the mainland, except they eventually give you back your gear after *they've* gone through it and wiped it. Option three—I borrow the laptop and we go through it. *Carefully*," he empha-

sized. "We remove what we need to remove, but you've still got ninety-five percent of what you had before and everything's in working order. In fact, in that scenario, you likely don't even know I'd been through your stuff."

He removed his hand from her mouth. "Now it's your turn."

"That covers my computer." She glared at him. "But I don't recall bringing my computer along on any of our dates. How about you explain *that* to me?"

He exhaled roughly. "Let's just say our original target has a brother who is really not happy with what happened to his family member. In fact, he's so unhappy that we had concerns about your personal safety, since it turns out you posted some of your lagoon photos before we could shut you down."

She blinked, the hurt and anger still simmering in her eyes. "I took photos of your operation?"

"That morning when I surprised you at the lookout point," he confirmed. "You got off a couple of shots of the Zodiacs coming in. There's enough detail there to make out our target's face. Fortunately, you didn't get any of my team. My team does a lot of covert ops." He cleared his throat. "It helps if the world doesn't know our faces. We go in, we blend in. That's why we were working as staff here on the island. It gave us a credible reason to be here, and most people don't look too closely at the staff."

"I don't even know you." She looked horrified. "Is Mason Black even your real name?"

This wasn't the woman who had been the most adventurous lover he'd ever had, who had opened her arms and her heart to him. He wanted that woman

back, because he was fairly certain she *did* know him in all the ways that mattered.

"That's me."

She wasn't done, though. "We don't really know any of the important details about each other. We know what each other likes in bed, but that's really it, isn't it?"

She steamed on ahead. "I don't know if you're a Republican or a Democrat. If you like quilted toilet paper or plain. Where your family lives, where you went to school, who your last girlfriend was and if your mom liked her."

Not sure how any of those things connected, he blurted out the first thing that came to mind. "My last girlfriend married me."

Her eyes widened. "So you *are* married."

"Not anymore. I was a kid, Maddie. I was eighteen when I got married and I was divorced by twenty."

Yeah. There was no missing the disgust written on her face, and he didn't think it was because she was worried about having committed adultery with him. "Do you have kids?"

"No." He leaned in. "No kids. No wife. Being a SEAL isn't a family-friendly activity. I'm gone for months at a time and there's always a chance that I'm not coming back." Meeting her gaze head-on, he added roughly, "Shit happens, Maddie, even on training runs. We push hard, live on the edge. There's a price tag on that kind of living, and it wasn't one my wife was willing to pay. I wasn't much better. I was still a kid. I hadn't figured out how to give her what she needed, and I thought a steady paycheck would be enough."

She thought about that for a moment. "How old are you?"

"Thirty-two." Although right now he felt as though he was pushing eighty. Or eight hundred.

"One last question."

Crap. Her voice caught on the last word as she moved to the closet and grabbed a bag. She needed more than he could give her right now, but he had no way of manufacturing more time.

"Shoot," he said, moving closer. Maybe if he could see her face, he could figure out the right thing to say. Find the words that would fix everything.

She swept her passport into her bag and turned around to face him. "Did I ever truly matter to you, or was I just convenient?"

There was absolutely nothing *convenient* about how he felt for her. Her face radiated pain and he…had a timeline.

"We need to move." And screw the mission. Leaning forward, he gently cupped her cheek. God, she was soft. And vulnerable. *All your fault, sailor.* "Yes, you did. You still do. But things are complicated right now."

She stiffened, the hollow expression on her face replaced by anger. "You're the security expert here, Mason, but I feel I need to make one thing perfectly clear."

Uh-huh. As long as she moved, she could say whatever she wanted. He owed her that and more. Cracking the door, he scanned their surroundings. So far, so good. It was a long shot that Santiago had made it back from the Belizean mainland only to ambush Maddie, but Mason wasn't taking chances.

"First, those words? Are the biggest cop-out ever. Second, I agree with you. We need to move on," she

said, allowing him to pull her out and onto the porch. "*I* need to move on. After you get me wherever it is we're going—"

"Naval cruiser about a mile off Fantasy Island," he responded, tucking her into his side and pulling her into the jungle. They'd cut through the trees to get to the beach, which would give them better cover.

"As soon as we set foot on deck," she spat, "we're done. Over. Kaput. *Finito*. Got it, soldier? Whatever game you've been playing with me is finished. I'm not part of your war games, and if there ever was an *us*, there isn't anymore."

"Understood," he said, because he did. He'd had his chance. He'd blown it. He and Maddie being anything more than a quick vacation hookup had been a fantasy, and fantasies stayed on Fantasy Island.

14

TONIGHT'S MISSION HAD been the SEAL version of ringing the doorbell and running. Mason's unit had been tapped to bring in one of the Marcos brothers' higher-profile lieutenants. The lieutenant, being neither stupid nor possessing a death wish, had gone to ground inside a compound just outside Belize City. The guy had played possum for so long that the higher-ups had started to wonder if he'd had another escape route planned and backdoored it out of the compound unseen. Mason and Levi had been charged with spooking the guy. Catch a ride on the Black Hawk, drop in and make a little noise. See if anyone startled and ran.

The chopper set down, hovering over the ground and kicking up a cloud of dust. The rotors chewed up the air, announcing their arrival with a loud *whap-whap-whap* only a dead man could have missed. He and Levi jumped down and started a quick run toward the compound walls.

"Maybe next time the CO will issue us cowbells," Levi quipped, stroking a hand down the barrel of his

cut-down grenade launcher. The man liked things that went boom a little too much sometimes.

"Or get us some instruments and we could lead the parade." Behind them, the Black Hawk lifted off. The pilot would make a few circles and be back to extract them in ten minutes, unless they discovered their target hiding inside.

Mason doubted it, though. The place was terminally sleepy, a small collection of run-down houses that didn't even qualify as a town. In addition to one small square that was little more than hard-packed dirt, there was a sorry-looking tree, a dilapidated church and one street. Set back two hundred yards from all that exciting action, the lieutenant's compound was the biggest, the windows covered with iron bars. It needed a paint job, though.

He got on the radio. "We got any signs of movement?"

"Negative" came the spotter's voice.

Okay, then.

He took a knee against the wall and looked at Levi. "You ready to ring the bell?"

"Hooyah." Levi flashed him a thumbs-up and then took aim, firing a stun grenade over the compound wall.

Lights flew on at the other houses. There were plenty of folks home there. Mason watched as the metal grille covering the nearest house slammed open, Mrs. Homeowner storming out to give someone a piece of her mind. She skidded to a halt four steps outside her door when the Black Hawk started to descend. A guy who was likely her husband came barreling out the door behind her, pulling on her arm to get her to back up.

"True love." Levi sighed as the couple retreated in-

side. "A woman like that would be perfect for us. Too bad we can't invite her along."

Mason did his job. He went in, he kicked ass, he pulled out. It was a nice, simple formula that worked for him. He'd never considered getting married again. His marriage with Bethany was proof enough that he wasn't husband material. He didn't check any of the boxes on those magazine quizzes about the perfect guy and the perfect husband.

But the perfect woman? He had a bad feeling that he'd watched her gorgeous ass storm away from him on a naval cruiser. As soon as he'd gotten Maddie to the ship waiting off the coast of Belize, she'd walked away without so much as a backward glance, a muttered curse or an attempt to get even. He'd seen SEAL teams take a stretch of sand with less determination. Her initial hurt and anger weren't unexpected, but her willingness to believe he cared for her? Yeah. That was a knee to the emotional balls he hadn't realized he'd grown. A woman hadn't made him think about playing for keeps since Bethany.

Which made this whole situation with Maddie difficult. He'd been pursuing her since he'd spotted her on Fantasy Island, and he wasn't good at the whole dating thing. In fact, he pretty much sucked at it. The sex was fantastic, but he was seriously out of practice at having a relationship. Maybe he should have been asking Gray for pointers, because the last he'd heard, his lieutenant commander was getting mighty serious with the surgeon he'd met on Fantasy Island.

Levi eyed him. "You gonna sulk all night? Or are you just striving for perfection as the strong, silent type?"

"Don't push your luck." He wasn't in the mood for Levi's brand of shit.

"Okay." Levi bumped his shoulder companionably. "Then, think less loudly about your AWOL girl, because your mental whining is louder than the skeeters they're growing down here, and it's clear Mr. Fantasy Fodder misses Maddie."

"I'm never living that down, am I?"

"In about a century." Levi sounded way too cheerful. "She took photos of your ass and shared them with ten thousand women. You're an internet sensation."

"I'm imagining introducing your head to my fists. Or the ground," he growled.

Levi, being Levi, didn't back off. Nope. He just wiggled his hips suggestively and kept right on talking as they sprinted toward the extract point. "You're gonna have to watch out for the paparazzi next time you're on the mainland. You'll have women stuffing dollar bills in your wetsuit."

"Maddie's better off without me," he said, because he wasn't touching Levi's vision of him as a male stripper.

His teammate blended into the shadows, dropping low as the Black Hawk started to drop overhead. "You bet. Santiago's neutralized and she's back on her home turf. She doesn't need a bodyguard. If I was the kind of guy who had feelings, though, I'd tell you I was worried about you."

Okay. Despite knowing that he should let her go because she deserved far better than his sorry ass, that didn't really make him feel any better. Bottom line? He couldn't stand the idea of losing her for good. *He* wanted to be with Maddie in ways that had nothing

to do with standing guard from the shadows and everything to do with that relationship he didn't know how to have.

"I don't know how to do this."

"Sure you do. You wait until the chopper is about two feet above the ground and then you run like hell, hoping the Marcos brothers haven't hired a team of snipers to shoot at your fine ass."

"Relationships," he gritted out, surveying their surroundings. Given the lack of welcoming gunfire, he doubted the lack of movement inside the compound was a decoy. "I'm completely out of practice at having one. Hell, I'm reading articles from girlie magazines."

"Actually, you're following the directions." From the gleeful expression on Levi's face, the other SEAL was enjoying this way too much.

"Screw you," he said, without heat, because Levi was right. It was kind of desperate, but this was Maddie... Apparently, he'd do whatever it took to win her. He hated the idea that he'd lost her.

"If we're getting our grade school on, I need to tell you that I think Maddie likes you. I should probably write it down and pass the note to you in study hall, but I'll give you the heads-up now since we're going to be busy extracting later on."

"She doesn't like *me*." Funny how that hurt. "She likes Mr. Fantasy Fodder, aka the guy pretending to be her perfect boyfriend based on a bunch of stupid magazine articles."

"Wake-up call." Levi forged ahead. "What did you do as the perfect boyfriend?"

"It's not as though we had a real relationship."

Levi grinned. "I'll try it a different way. Did Mr.

Fantasy Fodder do anything that Mason Black wouldn't have done?"

Mason opened his mouth. Closed it. Because the answer, honestly, was no.

"I'm betting not," Levi said quietly. "Which means it wasn't a lie, was it? You're still the same guy you were. She just had your job description wrong."

Damn it. Levi actually had a point. Just because he'd never done well in the relationship department didn't mean that what he and Maddie had had was any less real. It just wasn't something he'd been ready to slap a label on.

"SEALs and relationships don't mix." He and Bethany had learned that together.

"It's not easy." The carefree smile vanished from Levi's face. "It's tough as hell, actually. We both know that, but you've got family stateside. They're okay with waiting for you to come back, right? Maybe they'd rather have you full-time, but they understand you've got a job to do and that you're gonna be back when and if you can."

Yeah. He did. The emails always piled up in his account when he was on a mission, but they understood that he couldn't communicate while he ran an op. But all those emails were just words, while he missed the little moments. An inbox full of photos couldn't really make up for all of that.

"You think a woman like Maddie could do that?"

"There's only one way to find out. You have to put it to her, see what she says. *If* you want to keep her."

"Hooyah," he growled, because keeping Maddie was apparently all he could think about.

He put on a tough act and, most days, he *was* tough.

Tough like shoe leather, pizza that had been micro-waved ten minutes instead of ten seconds, tough like Levi's campfire steak. Sometimes, though, particularly when he checked those emails, saw those photos of his loved ones waiting for him back in San Francisco, he got a funny marshmallow feeling somewhere in his stomach.

Maddie was tough and funny—but she was also tremendously sweet and more than a little sentimental. She wrote about weddings and dresses, cakes and flowers and exotic honeymoons. All those things were about as foreign to him as clearing a compound in Afghanistan was to her. But he was willing to learn, not least because he enjoyed the hell out of her approach, both to cake and to life in general. She didn't hold back. At all. Her sexy little whimper of pleasure at the first bite made him think dirty thoughts about what else—okay, *who* else—might make her moan. Like *him*. He'd start with her thighs and…

"I want to keep her."

"Then, I highly recommend groveling." Levi moved, heading for the open door of the chopper. "Go after her. Beg. Tell her she's right, you're wrong and you'd like to spend the rest of your sorry life making it up to her."

It was a start. Mason jogged along behind him.

"When did you get so smart?"

The other man laughed and swung himself into the chopper. "I got married on Fantasy Island, remember?"

Right. That fucking perfect sunset and perfect moment on the beach. No way he'd forget that, or the way Maddie's face had lit up when he'd kissed her afterward. She made these husky moans when he *really* got her going, purely unforgettable. Yeah. He'd be happy

hearing those sexy sounds of hers again. Like once or twice a week, or once a day for the next forty years or so. The chopper lifted off, taking them away from the empty compound and their no-show target. BUD/S had prepared him for a compound full of hostiles, but nothing had prepared him for Maddie.

Groveling it was, just as soon as he could cart his sorry ass back to her.

15

Ladies, there is a reason Fantasy Island is all about fantasies. Fantasies are fun, but they're not real life. I screwed up big time. Let's just say that Mr. Fantasy Fodder was living a few fantasies of his own and he didn't share those fantasies with me. I'm feeling kind of stupid right now. All that hot kinkiness must have short-circuited something critical in my brain, because when I opened my mouth the last time I saw FF, *I asked him to marry me.* Stupid, stupid, stupid. It's time to stop hiding my head, though, because I've got another wedding this weekend. I'll be sure to report back to you with all the details about the wedding favors, the cake and the drunk groomsmen.

—MADDIE, Kiss and Tulle

THE WEDDING UNFOLDING in front of Maddie wasn't on an island, or even remotely tropical. The bride had gone with a purple palette and there probably wasn't a single orchid left in the entire state. She couldn't bring herself to care that the bride had employed ap-

proximately fourteen different shades of purple in her color scheme. It was ambitious. It was kind of an eyesore. And it didn't freaking matter, although the open bar was a plus.

The happy couple had waltzed down the aisle, and then the wedding guests had reassembled on the front lawn of what purported to be a fully functioning farm on a bona fide historic site. The big Victorian farmhouse looked more like a mansion, and most of the guests had booked rooms for the night. The bride had opted for a four-course dinner served under an enormous lilac tent, and fireworks would be shot off over nearby Lake Champlain when it got dark. As over-the-top fun as this particular wedding was, Maddie couldn't bring herself to care.

As the best man had brought the room to tears describing the groom's romantic proposal—something involving spelling out "Will you marry me?" in the snow with about two thousand tea lights—Maddie's own head was replaying a never-ending loop of her *own* proposal. Now that the embarrassment had faded, she missed Mason. Sure, she wanted to kick his fine butt, but she ached for him, too.

Stop thinking about the SEAL.

Waiters were clearing away the remains of the dinner, and the happy couple would be cutting the cake soon. Maddie had wandered over and taken a look at it earlier, snapping pictures of the four layers of purple-fondant goodness with crystalized violets. Her blog followers would definitely have an opinion on this one, and it was her duty to taste test it for them. After her Fantasy Island stay, her blog traffic was way up, and

she was finally bringing in enough money to keep both the lights and the water on.

"Where's your date, honey?" Maddie looked over at her neighbor because, even though she'd heard *that* particular question at least a half dozen times since she'd stepped out of the limo in her purple bridesmaid dress, it still sent a stab of pain through her.

The bride's aunt stared back at her expectantly. The elderly woman was almost swallowed up by the ruffles of her pastel dress, making it was clear where the bride had gotten her taste for colors from.

"I'm—" *Flying solo.* The words stuck in her throat.

"With me." The deep male voice behind her was all too familiar. She'd dreamed about the bastard every night since she'd left Fantasy Island three weeks ago. *Oh, no.* For a moment, she thought her mind was playing tricks on her, but when she turned around, Mason was standing there. He wore a white dress uniform with a chestful of medals, a dark-brimmed hat with a gold trident insignia tucked under his arm. Given the number of female heads turning his way, she wasn't hallucinating.

Maddie had no idea what to say to him. Her body didn't seem to share the same problem though, and was already leaning toward him. It probably made her pathetic, but her heart did an up-and-down leap in her chest, all the anger washing away. He'd dressed up. He'd come to the wedding. She didn't know what it meant, but he couldn't possibly be here by accident.

Her breath caught in her throat, wheezing from her lungs in a little gasp of surprise.

"Tell me you're not about to have an asthma attack,"

he said mildly. "Because that's the kind of thing that gives a guy a complex."

She sucked in a deep breath. Forced it out. "What are you doing here?"

"Dancing with you?" He held out a hand and she caved completely, letting him pull her out of her chair and onto the floor. For a few moments, they just danced, Mason smoothly navigating them around two giggling flower girls who were tossing leftover rose petals at the dancers' feet and an usher who had already hit the open bar too hard. The dancing was one of her favorite parts of the reception, everybody getting up and cutting loose because they were happy, there was music and it was always a good day when two people were willing to stand up and tell the whole world how much they loved each other. It also didn't matter if you couldn't dance or had no sense of rhythm, because you could get lost in the bobbing, weaving sea of tulle and poorly glued sequins.

He tugged on one of the ribbon straps holding up her dress. "Nice color."

She didn't want to talk about her dress.

"Why are you here?" And why was she dancing with him?

"Can I show you something?"

"Is that code for something dirty?" Instinctively, she fell back into the sexy banter they'd shared on the island. She'd kind of used up her honesty quota when she'd proposed to him.

He stared at her somberly. "Not yet," he said, and she wasn't sure if she was disappointed or not. Instead, he maneuvered her to the edge of the dance floor and then out of the reception tent altogether. It was almost dark, the stars popping out in the sky overhead. He

walked her over the lawn, toward the formal gardens that edged the woods. The rich scent of roses and lavender filled the air. Purple aside, the bride had picked a gorgeous spot for a wedding.

"So," she murmured. "You wanted to play show-and-tell?"

Because they were a long way from Fantasy Island, whatever he wanted to show her had to be good. He dropped her hand and shrugged out of his dress jacket. When he handed it to her, she couldn't stop herself from smoothing the fabric with her fingertips, the material warm from his skin. She shrugged into the jacket, trying to tamp down the feeling of anticipation spreading through her. Maybe he'd just stopped by to say hello. Two thousand miles from where he'd last seen her.

It was possible. Lots of things were possible.

"You really are a SEAL."

He shot her a look. "Yeah. I am."

It fit him—and it also explained a lot. Things like the way he moved with such purpose, and his confidence underwater. The way he'd pinned her so effortlessly when she'd surprised him sleeping. While he went to work on his sleeve, unbuttoning the cuff, she asked the question that had been bothering her.

"So you're not a chef?"

"I love to cook." A slow smile tugged at his mouth. "I wasn't kidding about the four sisters. They loved to eat. I loved to make them happy."

He shoved his sleeve up and held his arm out. Black and pink—*pink*—words scrolled across his inner forearm: "That's how much I love you." He'd finished the

Ogden Nash poem inked on her hip. Her heart gave a pathetic little stutter while other parts of her melted.

"I looked up the rest of your poem," he said gruffly. "And I thought I needed to tell you that's how much I love you, too."

Too. She ran her fingers lightly over his skin. The tattoo had healed, so he must have done it almost as soon as she'd left.

"But you don't like needles." Stupid.

He shook his head. "No. I don't. But I like you. Hell, Maddie, read the words. I more than like you."

She kept waiting to wake up, because she'd had some pretty awesome dreams about him these past few weeks, but she didn't, and reality was apparently better than anything she could concoct on her own. "You have to say it or it doesn't count."

He pulled her up against him. "Is that so? Because I want you back, and you should know that I'm willing to do whatever it takes. Tell me I'm not too late."

"That's a good start."

"I'm sorry, sweetheart. I'm sorry it took me longer than it did you to figure out that what we have is something rare and truly special. I'm sorry I made you propose first, when I should have known it was a privilege to love you and that I was a crazy fool to let you go when I could have held on." He tightened his arms around her. "How am I doing so far?"

"You're getting warmer. Keep going."

"We're supposed to be together. I love you and I'll do whatever it takes to prove that to you." He swept her backward into a deep, passionate kiss that rocked her world. Rocked her heart.

Long minutes later, when he broke off their kiss and

rested his forehead against hers, she felt too much. The emotions rushing through her made her heart swell and bang against her rib cage. Mason had come for her.

"One more thing," he said.

"Okay." Why had he stopped? And *why* was he still talking?

"I'm a US Navy SEAL."

Yeah. She could see that for herself. "Kind of showed me back there on the island," she reminded him.

"It's who I am," he continued thickly. "I don't know if I'll serve for five years or fifty, but it's part of me, part of who I am. I need to know you're good with that."

"Waiting for you?" God. He was going to have to yell his answer, because her heart was thundering in her ears.

He held her gaze, as though her next words were more important than any mission go. "Yes. In our bed, in our house. I'd like to tell you that we'll figure it out, that it maybe gets easier with time and with practice, but I don't know. I've never had to be the one waiting and it's every bit as hard as being the guy out there in the field."

With the guns and the danger. She didn't like thinking about Mason getting hurt or being out there where things like Santiago Marcos happened on a daily basis. What she did know, though, was that she absolutely, 200 percent wanted to be the woman he came home to.

"We've got this," she said finally. "Just as long as you swear you'll always come home."

"I promise." His breath shuddered out, as if he'd been holding it and doing some waiting of his own. "And I accept your proposal, if it's still good. I didn't hear an expiration date, and you're going to have to cut

me some slack for being slow. Let me marry you and I'll be the happiest goddamned SEAL ever."

MADDIE TEARED UP. She stared at him and he could see—*see*—the tears welling up in her eyes. Crap. "You're not supposed to cry."

Not sure how to fix this, he hauled her close, letting her blubber all over his dress shirt. She already had his jacket and his heart. She could have everything else, too.

She pressed a hand against his chest. "You're in uniform."

"Yeah." He looked back at her steadily. "This didn't seem like a T-shirt affair, and you're worth getting dressed up for."

"Or naked," she said hopefully.

"Or naked," he agreed. He suddenly had a whole new appreciation for how the animals felt at the zoo. He'd liberated a palace's worth once in the Middle East, busting the locks on the cages and letting the beasts free. It had seemed like the right thing to do, then and now, because with an entire sea of unfamiliar faces staring at him from an enormous purple tent, he felt the same way. Plus, he itched just looking at the clothes. This wasn't his kind of scene.

What Maddie was wearing wasn't so bad, however. Apparently, she'd lucked out in the bridesmaid sweepstakes this time. Her blueberry-pie-colored dress was made out of a floaty fabric that brushed the floor, and it had those skinny spaghetti straps that seemed too thin to hold up her gorgeous breasts. He had plans for those straps, like thumbing them off her shoulder. Not that he'd get too far, because the top of her dress was

a little snug and they spilled over the top, tempting him to touch. She looked ravishing, even if her hair had been pinned up in an elaborate series of curls and braids. He'd probably stormed beaches in less time than it had taken to do her hair.

She sniffed.

He hadn't fixed anything, hadn't fixed them. "Don't cry. I'll make this right."

White knighting was dangerous. He sucked at being a hero. He was also, apparently, a sucker for her curves. When she looked at him, her beautiful brown eyes gleaming with mischief, he felt it right down to the toes of his dress shoes.

"I'm happy," she whispered, and then she launched herself at him again. "I love you, too." When they finally came up for air, however, she'd thought of another question. "How did you get here?"

For a moment, his tongue got stuck and he felt more than a little light-headed. That happened when he was around Maddie. Nothing he could ever do would be enough to earn her love and the privilege of standing by her side. She was giving it to him, though, giving herself to him, and he planned to spend every minute of the next eighty years proving to her that she'd made the right call. She was his everything. It was that fucking simple, so he ought to be able to answer her question.

"Motorcycle." He jerked a thumb toward the entrance of the fancy pavilion thingie. A guy in a uniform had offered to "Valet this for you, sir?" But he'd declined, because he liked to keep his lines of retreat open.

She glowed up at him as he steered her through the tent, where the reception he'd crashed was being held. Coming in uniform had its advantages, because

the valets and the lady with the headset running the op hadn't questioned him. He'd do whatever it took to keep that look of happiness on Maddie's face. As they moved through the crowd of guests, he focused on the exit. He wanted to get her out of here. Partly because he wanted to find out what she had on under that dress, but more because he was ready to get on with *them*.

She elbowed him. "Are we leaving?"

"You want to go for a ride?" *Say yes.* He'd wait out the reception if that was what she wished, but they were definitely eloping when it was their turn. He wasn't starring in any dinner-dance spectacle.

"Can I drive?" She looked up at him hopefully.

"The keys are in my pocket." She looked good in his jacket. Maybe he could convince her to wear just the jacket later on. She fished in the pocket for the keys— and came up with both the keys and a little black box.

"That's for you," he said. That damn magazine article had better have been right, or he'd go hunt down the writer personally.

She opened the box. He'd spotted the ring in the jeweler's window. It was bold and blingy, with enough carats to blind someone from across the room. The ring had pizzazz and it made him smile. Maybe he should have let her pick out her own ring. Waiting until she'd said yes might have been smart, too.

"I read on a blog that proposals should be memorable," he said when she didn't say anything. Her fingers patted the velvet sides, stroked over the stones. He didn't hear a no. In fact, he didn't hear anything at all.

She lifted her head and looked at him, a mixture of emotions on her face. Amusement, pleasure—and something he really hoped looked a whole lot like love.

"Then, go ahead and make it," she said. She didn't let go of the box, though. Or throw it at him. So he went for broke and dropped to one knee on the grass, taking the hand that wasn't holding the ring box.

"Madeline Holmes, will you marry me? Not saying yes when you proposed to me was one of the biggest mistakes of my life. I shouldn't have let you go."

He was pretty sure that they had an audience watching them from the big purple tent—an audience with cell phones. They'd be starring front and center on YouTube, and that was okay by him. He wasn't sure, however, how long he was supposed to spend on bended knee. The magazine article had been annoyingly vague on that part. He settled for tugging her down onto his thigh. She leaned into him and grinned.

"I was moving kind of fast."

He smiled. Maddie only seemed to have two speeds: gung-ho and full steam ahead. She didn't hold back, either, in bed or in matters of the heart. There was a lot he could learn from her. He'd made a mistake when he'd been eighteen, and he'd been scared of repeating it. Instead, he'd made a different mistake, letting go when he should have held on.

"Yes," she said.

"Yes?" He was pretty certain his heart was on his sleeve for everyone to see, and he needed to get this right.

"Yes, you can slide that pretty ring of yours on my finger." She pressed a kiss against his mouth. "Does that mean I don't have to buy *you* a ring?"

"Hell no." He fished the ring out of the box, praying he didn't drop it. He didn't need a magazine article to know that fishing around in the grass for Maddie's

diamonds wasn't the ending he was shooting for. "I insist on a ring."

"All right." Her smile promised the best kind of trouble. "We can negotiate where I put it later. When we don't have an audience."

His heart did a funny little flop. "I love you, sweetheart," he repeated, because he couldn't say it too much. "Tell me you know that."

"I do." She laced her fingers behind his head, hanging on to him for all she was worth. "And I'll say that again anytime you want."

Ladies, this is Maddie's Mr. Fantasy Fodder reporting in. You're going to have to share her with me, because now that my fantasy woman's let me put a ring on her finger, we've got big plans. Maddie mentioned a few fantasies that need filling, and I'm honored to serve. Since she's out wrangling a few wedding cakes for us to taste test, I'm taking over for the day, and I've got your quiz for you.

How do you know you've met the woman of your dreams?

A) You walk up to the bar and order a *Honey, I Dew* martini in front of your entire SEAL team. Those boys have long memories, but there's no reason not to make her happy. Plus, she ordered up a round of *Leather and Lace* shots for them.

B) You tell everyone you meet all about her. So much so that your lieutenant commander announces that if loose lips sank ships, you've taken out the entire US

Navy. She's basically like a supersmart, really sexy supermodel that took a chance on your dumb ass. Hello, who wouldn't brag about that?

C) You know you need to wake up and kiss her first thing in the morning for the next fifty years—and the 18,000th kiss will be every bit as good as the first.

—MADDIE's MASON, *Kiss and Tulle*

* * * * *

Watch for the next book in Anne Marsh's series,
DARING HER SEAL, *coming May 2016,*
only from Harlequin Blaze!